Praise for Ron Faust

"Faust's prose is as smooth and bright as a sunlit mirror."
—*Publishers Weekly*

"Hemingway is alive and well and writing under the name Ron Faust."

—Ed Gorman, author of *Night Kills*

"Faust is one of our heavyweights ... you can't read a book by Ron Faust without the phrase 'major motion picture' coming to mind."

—Dean Ing, *New York Times* bestselling author of *The Ransom of Black Stealth One*

"Faust writes of nature and men like Hemingway, with simplicity and absolute dominance of prose skills."

—Bill Granger, award-winning author of *Hemingway's Notebook*

"He looms head and shoulders above them all—truly the master storyteller of our time. Faust will inevitably be compared to Hemingway."

—Robert Bloch, author of *Psycho*

D0366194

RON FAUST

DEATH FIRES

A TOM DOHERTY ASSOCIATES BOOK
NEW YORK

This is a work of fiction. All the characters and events portrayed in this book are either products of the author's imagination or are used fictitiously.

DEATH FIRES

Cover art by Cliff Nielsen

A Forge Book
Published by Tom Doherty Associates, Inc.
175 Fifth Avenue
New York, NY 10010

Forge® is a registered trademark of Tom Doherty Associates, Inc.

ISBN: 0-812-53533-2

First Forge edition: December 1997

Printed in the United States of America

0 9 8 7 6 5 4 3 2 1

About, about, in reel and rout
The death-fires danced at night;
The water, like a witch's oils,
Burnt green, and blue and white.

Coleridge
The Rime of the Ancient Mariner

prologue

In early May some members of a dune buggy club discovered the mutilated bodies of two women in the Mohave Desert northeast of Los Angeles. A forensic pathologist stated that they had died of multiple knife wounds; there were thirty-three stab and slash wounds on one body, twenty-six on the other. And the women had been decapitated and their hands severed at the wrists. The missing parts were not found; the bodies never identified. The pathologist also reported that both women had engaged in intercourse around the time of their deaths. They might very well have been prostitutes, the police said; prostitutes were often the victims of such insanely vicious crimes.

It was a front-page story in the Los Angeles newspapers for several days, moved back to page two, three, and finally vanished altogether. There were new crimes every day; slashers, arsonists, stranglers, snipers, bombers, poisoners—and the public lost interest in what the Hearst paper called the "Mohave Misses."

But before the story died, a psychiatrist was quoted as saying that the American people were becoming inured to violence, losing their capacity to feel and act as a mutually supportive community. "We are all islands now."

A priest said that these were the times of the Antichrist.

A rabbi claimed that the fascist mentality was taking the tactics and morality of Auschwitz out into the American streets.

A police captain said that we needed more cops, tougher laws, tougher judges, longer sentences, tougher prisons, tougher parole boards, busier gallows and electric chairs and gas chambers. "It's them or us," he said.

o n e

. . . *and the young man had forgotten exactly when he had gone swimming with the sharks. He had written a few lines in the logbook afterward, but it was undated.*

> *Once I floated among the yellow salt weed,*
> *balanced between sea and sky,*
> *while sharks flew in parabolas*
> *and grinned at clown-striped pilot fish.*

The sharks had not been aggressive; they seemed as lethargic as all the other marine creatures here—as he himself was. Consequence had been severed from action.
He spent most of his days in the shade of the cockpit awning, studying the strange animals that lived among the sargasso weed: ten foot long sea-worms with thistle

heads; paper-thin white fish that exploded into confetti if he touched them with a boathook; transparent fish with clearly visible skeletons and organs; suction-headed eels; jellyfish more delicately beautiful than orchids; lizardlike fish with overdeveloped pectoral fins, which they used to crawl through the weeds like lazy amphibians; plants that appeared to be animals and animals that looked like plants—not a day passed that he didn't see something queer and wonderful.

At night the sea sparkled with bioluminescence, flashing here and there with a cold, green fire. At night, too, he noticed that all around the horizon a thin, blue radiance burned as if it were still daylight just beyond the limits of his vision. And at night, before the batteries were drained, he used to listen to the radio; sometimes he heard voices urgently speaking German and Spanish and Portuguese, but more often the radio emitted curious hums and keens and purrs and whistles—it was like a new kind of electronic music.

He wrote letters to the world and posted them in bottles that remained drifting alongside the boat.

One day he saw a girl in a large yellow life raft. He gazed at her through the binoculars. She was thin and sunburned, with cracked lips, and hair that had been bleached snow white by the sun. The next morning she was still out there.

Sometimes he tried to obtain his position by sun and lunar and star sights, but they never worked out. It was strange. The sextant was not damaged. He certainly could not question the H.O. 214 tables. Still, every time he worked out a sight the result was ridiculous; they placed him in the center of the Mato Grosso or near the Seychelles or well up on the slopes of Mt. Kenya. He wondered if the air here refracted light in such a way that it became impossible to take an accurate sight. Per-

haps, in some inexplicable way, he was sighting on mirages. Absurd. Yet the atmosphere was peculiar here; bright, pellucid, but with a certain indefinable density— it did really seem that the light was penetrating something far more viscid than air.

Not that it mattered.

He was possessed by a heat-drugged indifference. It was not apathy. He was not bored or unhappy. It was mostly a kind of sensual indolence, a half sleep. He felt himself submitting to timeless time and unintelligible space.

The sky tilted and a shadow absorbed the sun. Night now, the stars shining like backlighted gems, violet and blue and amber, and dim electric-blue fires raging all around the horizon.

One morning he came up on deck and saw that the yellow life raft was only a few yards off the port beam. The girl shyly turned away from his stare. She was starving. Her joints looked disproportionately large, and he could see her skull, a death's head, outlined beneath her sun-blistered skin. Her arms and legs were spotted with raw, red sores. At dusk the raft was still there.

The compass behaved queerly. Often, when the boat was motionless on a sea as calm and hard-looking as a mineral plain, the compass card would begin to move. Slowly, evenly, it revolved degree by degree, and once it shifted a full three hundred and sixty degrees before finally stabilizing.

The next morning when he awakened he saw that the girl was sleeping in the port settee berth. She shivered and whimpered, and once cried out, "They're all gone! All dead!" Her belly was distended. She had drunk too much water.

He thought that he should check to see how much water remained in the tanks, but his mind wandered, he *lost the impulse, and instead he went up on deck to tease the sea animals with a boat hook.*

Julian tossed the script into the top desk drawer and slammed the drawer closed. This was the third time he had tried to read the script, and he had not been able to get past the sleeping girl. It didn't tell him anything; it didn't indicate how he was supposed to do his job.

Michael Callaghan, the second cameraman, was equally confused. Yesterday, while they had been eating shrimp in the restaurant patio, he had told Julian that a dozen more pages into the script a German submarine captain appeared. The submariner had apparently been drifting around the horse latitudes since the Second World War. At that point, Callaghan said, a weird story turned more or less psychotic.

"How are we supposed to film this surrealistic crap, Julian?" he asked now.

"I don't know."

"It's so goddamned subjective. How do we film this guy submitting to timeless time and unintelligible space?"

"I don't know. I suppose DiMotta does." Alfredo DiMotta, an Argentine of Italian extraction, was the author of the script and would direct the movie.

"How are we going to film this punk's sensual indolence?"

"I don't know, Mick."

Callaghan was about sixty years old, small boned, with white hair and eyebrows, watery blue eyes, and pale skin flushed with masses of wormy, broken blood vessels. Julian had once liked and respected Callaghan, learned from him; but the man was a drunk now and a difficult companion.

"How are we going to film the density of the light? Got an idea about that, pal?"

Julian shook his head.

"Why couldn't he give us a regular shooting script instead of this novelistic treatment?"

"I guess that's the way DiMotta likes to work. He writes for mood and then improvises a lot during the shooting. Now why don't we drop this."

"You've met our boy Alfredo, haven't you?" Callaghan asked, looking at Julian in a certain way. It was a glance of skepticism, humor, as if he had deliberately elicited a lie; and it contained a kind of sly complicity. It was a look that had become familiar to Julian in recent months. He often saw it on the faces of his friends, and it informed him that they knew something that he should know and did not. More; that perhaps he really did know and was lying. "Well?" Callaghan said.

"No, I haven't met him."

Callaghan nodded as if accepting Julian's answer, but that blandly conspiratorial look remained.

"I have," Callaghan said. "Ever see any of his pictures?"

"No. But I hear that he's seriously regarded in Europe and South America."

"Yeah? Seriously regarded? For what?"

"He's considered an artist."

Callaghan grinned, lifted his eyebrows, leaned forward over the table, and said, "Oh, well . . . Yes, I see, an *artist*. Hell, I had no idea—what was that you said? An *artist?*"

Julian smiled.

"That changes everything. I'm content now, Julian. I really am so honored to be working on this weird low-budget picture that stars a couple of TV rejects and is directed by . . . What was that you said? An artist? How can I convey, ah, my enthusiasm?''

"Let's give DiMotta a chance," Julian said.

"Indeed!"

"We're working, Mick. It's been a while since either of us has worked."

"Indeed, indeed," Callaghan said. He lit a cigarette, again looked at Julian with doubt and complicity. "Listen, pal, you do know that the artist DiMotta is a pornographer."

Julian shook his head.

"In addition to his, ah, artistic cinema, he turns out porn films. Classy porn, fine technically, clean-looking orgiastics, but still porn."

"How do you know that, Mick?"

"You might, perhaps, have seen one of his porn flicks at one time or another." The look again.

"Why would he take a chance on ruining his reputation by making pornographic pictures?"

"He doesn't put his name on the screen, for Christ's sake."

"But I'm asking you, why would he take the chance?"

"Money, Julian. He might do it for the money. Is that an alien concept? Money. And maybe he does it for the sport, too. For the benefit of his libido. I don't know, I'm just telling you that the new darling of *Cahiers du Cinéma* makes porn flicks."

"I'll ask you again—how do you know?"

"I know. You know also. You damned well know it. But let's have another drink. And something more to eat. What about the crab?"

"You haven't finished your shrimp."

"I don't like food, kid, just the idea of food."

That was yesterday. Now Julian got up from the desk,

went into the bathroom, and drew a glass of water from the faucet, and then returned to the big room. The water was cloudy and tasted sour. He drank it slowly, like medicine. There was a breeze coming in through the screened windows and the noontime desert heat—dry and light, herbal-scented—had given him another headache.

The temperature was now about ninety-five degrees. And even though he would be able to throw a stone into the sea from outside his cabaña door, he guessed that the humidity could not be much above twenty-five percent. It was difficult for him to believe that the sea was so near unless he was looking at it. The odor was not strong, and there was rarely any sound. Julian was used to the rich iodine smells of the sea along the California coast, and the incessant thunder of breaking ground swells. Here the water was glass-smooth, burnished a blinding silver by the sun in daylight and looking like molten asphalt at night. He had not seen any waves big enough to be called surf.

He closed the windows, turned on the air conditioner, and then got dressed; a polo shirt, tennis shorts, and sandals. He carefully avoided the mirrors as he moved around the cottage. It was not that his scars were disfiguring; the surgeon who had placed the sutures had done a superb job. The scars were thin centipedes now, but in another year or two they would be no more noticeable than his natural frown and laugh lines. The scars did not bother him; they hardly altered his image. But he did not like to see the new expression on his face, or what he imagined to be a new expression. He saw doubt when he looked at himself, and a kind of bewilderment— something not far from anguish. He saw a face that always seemed on the verge of wincing.

Julian had been an extremely fortunate man for thirty-six years, and then, in just a few seconds, misfortune finally caught up with him and more than evened the score. He'd experienced seventy years of bad luck in the time it takes to smile and say, "Yes." And now, eighteen months later, he still was not finished counting his losses. "Not all of the precincts have reported," he'd told one of the doctors.

He had been a kind of small-time golden boy; bright, athletic, good-looking, moderately talented, lucky, and with that physical and mental health that unhappy people choose to regard as stupidity. But now he saw himself as just another casualty. And he yearned for his lost health as a fallen priest might yearn for lost faith.

two

When Julian stepped outside, the sun-glare momentarily blinded him, spread a dark film over his vision. His head ached. He retreated into the shade of a coconut palm, and after a few seconds the film vanished and he could see the long main lodge and the other cabañas—white cubes with red tile roofs—tucked away here and there among the trees. This was a tiny oasis in an all but dead land; there were coconut and date palms, fig trees, lime and lemon and olive trees, orange and papaya.

But beyond these forty or fifty acres there was little other than sandy reddish soil, rocks and stones, stunted cacti, thorny brush, and bare, furrowed mountains—you looked back over the desert to those mountains and wondered how long ago there had been rain enough to erode them that way.

Ahead was the glittering light-faceted sea; and several miles offshore a steep, rocky island—*Isla Seca*—and farther still, the thin seam that joined the cerulean sky to the ice-blue sea. A few gulls glided along the beach, tilting their wings to exploit the random breaths of air.

It was silent now except for the mewing of the gulls and the regular thumping of the big diesel engines that provided power for electricity and the small desalinization plant. The engines were located in another cubical white building on the southern edge of the orchard. They ran twenty hours a day. After Julian's first three days here he did not often consciously notice the muted pounding of the engines, but he believed that he was always aware of it in the lower levels of thought. He had told a doctor, a sport fisherman down from Phoenix, that it seemed that his heartbeat had altered its rhythm slightly in response to the throbbing engines. The doctor had laughed and said, "Absurd, nothing to that at all." Still, Julian continued to awaken in a vague panic when the engines stopped at 2:00 A.M.

Now he left the shade and walked through the trees toward the main building. He jumped an irrigation ditch, passed the salt water swimming pool (fresh water was precious here), and walked around the tennis court.

The court had been made with a reddish clay—local clay, perhaps—that had cracked and buckled in the heat. You could not get a clean bounce off that surface.

He passed between two cabañas and then climbed over a driftwood fence. Two workmen, eating lunch in the shade of a palm, nodded and murmured, *"Buenos días."* Julian went down the side of the main building, turned the corner, and walked past a series of doors, motel rooms, a gift shop, an office, a tackle shop, a package liquor store.

He entered the restaurant. There were twenty tables with red and white checked tablecloths, a long bar running the length of the west wall, and many billfish hanging on the rattan-matted walls. One was a black marlin that weighed, so he had been told, nearly nine hundred pounds when caught. All of the fish looked like lacquered foam and plastic fakes now; they didn't seem to have anything in common with real fish. The morticians and taxidermists keep trying, but there is really no way of making a dead animal look like a living one, Julian thought. He studied the marlin for a moment and thought about how great the fish must have been while in the sea, how swift and powerful, one of nature's monarchs; and how pathetic it was as a wall ornament.

It was twelve-thirty now, but the fishermen usually stayed out all day on the boats, and so the dining room was nearly empty. Tomás, the ancient maitre d', handed Julian a letter, shuffled his menus and looked around anxiously, as if doubtful about securing a place this afternoon, and then, suddenly inspired, led the way to one of the seventeen empty tables.

When the waiter came, Julian ordered a bottle of Bohemia beer, a bowl of fish soup, and a steak sandwich.

A man sitting at a nearby table was staring at him. He nodded when Julian returned his gaze and then, smiling, looked down at his hands.

The letter was from DiMotta. Julian tore open the envelope and removed two sheets of onionskin paper. He could see, peripherally, that the man was staring at him again. He turned.

The man smiled. "How have you been?" He had a deep, mellow voice and what might have been an English accent. Perhaps he was in films, an actor, someone that Julian might have met.

"Fine," Julian said. "And you?"

"Lovely," the man said, and then he laughed softly, breathlessly. "I'm so pleased to see you again." He nodded several times. "So nice, really."

Even though the man was seated, Julian could see that he was very tall. And very thin; his cream-colored suit jacket hung over his wide shoulders as if there were no flesh beneath, just the frame of bones. He was probably in his early seventies. He had long white hair, grayish waxy-looking skin that was sheened with sweat, a long jaw, a wide pink-lipped mouth (rouged lips?), a horny beak of nose, and gray eyes tucked back in dark hollows. His hands were big, square, with long yellow fingernails.

"The food is good here," he said. "Yes, I'm happy about that. I was afraid that I would have to eat tortillas and frijoles and enchiladas and horrible sticky things like that."

Julian did not reply.

"I was told that I would see you here, James."

"My name isn't James."

He laughed silently. "Of course it isn't."

Julian unfolded the letter.

Dear Julian:

I am so glad you consented to join me in this small adventure. (I regard my films as adventures, existential inquiries during which the answers pose some intriguing questions—does that sound pretentious?) I admire your work and I'm certain that we will get on very well together. I ask that my cast and crew be creative, that they bring the deepest parts of themselves to my project, that they gamble with their pain and inhibition, empty themselves, dare to be free. Again, this sounds pretentious, but what I mean to say is that the best parts of my pictures have always been those that were conceived and executed in a kind of frenzied improvisation.

I vainly describe them as my films, but they are really our films, a collaborative effort whose value is ideally in the making and not the viewing, the total experience and not the result. If people happen to enjoy the result (the edited film), fine—if they despise it, also fine. Do you see? The film will be the refuse of the moment, an inferior representation of previously vital emotions. All of this is to say that you are welcome to seize the reins should you be possessed by inspiration.

I may be delayed here in Los Angeles for another week. Please continue to look for potential locations and, when the equipment and film arrives, begin on your own to record background and atmospheric footage.

I am thinking specifically of the empty sea, the circular and therefore infinite horizon, the stars and sun, solitude, desolation, the abstract horror of vacuity. An absence is far more frightening than any presence, don't you agree?

Try shooting with different types of film, with various lenses and filters, etc., at dismal hours of the day and night—remember only that I desire a visual analogue of spiritual deprivation. Our helpless mariners are perhaps the equivalent of astronauts who have somehow become adrift in space, separated from all that has meaning to the race. Humans deprived of their home, earth, and of all their elaborate illusions, i.e., comfort, culture, morality, civilization, conventional time, etc. Stress, terrible stress. Raw animals once more. Reduced to dumb beasts ultimately. A similiar situation is more likely to occur today in our great industrial cities, among the crowds, amidst plenty, but I believe that this—call it alienation,

malaise, whatever—can be more effectively conveyed in
a wilderness.

But here, in trying to be vague I have become specific.
In the act of offering you freedom I have denied it. Go
and do as you like. If you are inventive enough, strong
enough or weak enough, this adventure will turn into
your odyssey. You will guide all of us into your labyrin-
thine self. (Or perhaps it will be one of the others. We
shall see.) Such journeys are not completed without suf-
fering.

> *With confidence and hope,*
> *Alfredo DiMotta*

Julian folded the letter, returned it to the envelope,
and lit a cigarette. He hoped that DiMotta in person was
not as goofy as he seemed in the letter.

The tall man was staring at Julian again. "Your letter
was from Alfredo, wasn't it?" he asked. "Forgive me,
please, but I recognized the handwriting. Alfredo writes
a beautiful, old-fashioned hand, doesn't he? It's almost
calligraphy. You've met Alfredo, haven't you?"

Julian shook his head.

"But I thought . . . at one of my parties . . ."

"No."

"But surely . . ."

The waiter brought Julian's soup, the bottle of beer,
and a basket of hard rolls.

"Surely, James, you must remember those nights."

"My name isn't James."

"Oh, please, I know. I was only teasing. Stupid me.
No harm in it. I'm sorry, really I am."

The man had a pleasantly ugly face, a V-shaped smile,
a gentle and resonant voice, easy manners—and Julian
despised him. He seemed to offer an obscure insinuation

with every word, each glance. He was courteous and yet he indirectly violated the intent of courtesy. He bypassed all of the usual codes and barriers and established a kind of dirty intimacy.

Now he slowly rose to his feet, picked up his wide-brimmed Panama hat, and smiled again. "The soup is superb. You'll have a lovely lunch, I know."

Julian did not speak.

The man placed the Panama hat on his head at a jaunty angle, tugged at the brim with thumb and forefinger, and then picked up his walking stick. It was made out of twisted black wood and had a triangular iron ferule and a gold serpent's-head grip. He was about six feet seven or eight inches tall, very thin, with a long neck and a prominent Adam's apple. The skin on his face and neck was finely wrinkled, like crepe paper. He had obviously lost a great deal of weight since his suit had been tailored; it hung loosely on his frame, bagged around his middle and buttocks. He had once been a giant; now he was only very tall.

"I won't call you James ever again," he said. "I promise."

Julian nodded.

"It was a little joke between us—you remember. But really, it's been so nice seeing you again. You look fit, you honestly do. I hope you don't suffer from those horrid headaches anymore."

He sighed then, tapped his cane three times on the floor, murmured, "Damn entropy," and started stiffly toward the door. "It was a splendid lunch, Tomás," he called to the maître d'. "Thank you so much. I'll attend to all gratuities on Friday of each week. Good day now." He paused at the door, shifted the walking stick to his left hand, twisted the doorknob with his right, and just before leaving, he glanced back at Julian over his shoulder. He was smiling a pink, satyr's V-smile, and his eyebrows were arched high over his deeply set eyes. Then he was gone.

Julian glanced at his table; despite all the talk of fine food, he had hardly eaten; a half glass of wine, a bite or two of fish, half of the salad. The soup and bread appeared untouched. A cigar stub smoldered in the abalone shell ashtray.

A repellent man. There was something dry, scaly, slow—reptilian—about him. But Julian did not doubt that they had met, or that he had attended the parties, or even that he might have met DiMotta at one of them.

Eighteen months ago Julian had been in an automobile accident and had been badly hurt; a skull fracture, internal injuries, six broken bones, compressed vertebrae . . . (Even so, he had been the "lucky" one; three passengers in his car had been killed.) He had been in the hospital for three months, was a semi-invalid for months more, and during a period of about six weeks last spring (when he believed that he had finally recovered his health), he had experienced severe headaches and intermittent blackouts—"fugue states", a doctor had called them. There had been five such fugues, none lasting more than ten or eleven hours; but during them he had met people he could not now remember, done and said things he could not now recall, been an almost sinister stranger to himself.

It had terrified him. It still did. Fugues, serial amnesia—he was not comforted by the knowledge that science had names for those lost intervals.

After lunch he walked down a hall past the restrooms and a storeroom to the back office. The door was open and Duane Poole, co-owner of the resort, was sitting behind his big teak desk. His eyes were closed. He was tapping a pencil point on the desk blotter.

"Duane?" Julian said.

He looked up. "What? Oh, Julian, come on in. I was only considering suicide. Red ink again last month, lots of it."

Julian entered the office and sat down. "This should be a good month, with the movie company here."

"It'll help. Want a cold one?"

"No, thanks."

Duane Poole was about forty, with kinky orange hair and greenish eyes and a square face blotched with freckles and old acne scars. He and his partner, a Tijuana lawyer, had recently bought the resort. They were not doing very well.

"There was a man in the restaurant I haven't seen before," Julian said. "Rather, I don't remember meeting him. Very tall, very thin. Cream-colored tropical suit, Panama hat, walking stick—a strange man. He looks like he's been dead a week or so."

"Oh, yeah."

"Who is he?"

"You mean to say you don't know him?"

"That's right."

"The guy talked like he knew you. Almost like you were old pals."

"Well, just who the hell is he?"

"He's the man with the bucks."

"Look, do we have to play twenty questions?"

"Saukel—he's the money man of the picture. The producer."

"Christ," Julian said.

"Frederick Saukel."

"I'll probably kill him within the week."

"He seems like a nice old guy."

"Does he, Duane?"

"Kind of sweet."

"Is that right?"

"I guess he's American, but he acts like an old world type."

"Really?"

"What's wrong with you?" Duane asked.

"He must have come in on the morning shuttle plane. Was there anyone with him?"

"I'll say there was. A beautiful girl, a goddess of the silver screen, maybe. And a guy, the star, Neil something, and three creepy kids that Saukel calls his hominids. What I want to know, Julian—what are hominids?"

"I think it's an anthropologist's term for early near-man, pre-man, close to human."

"They didn't look very close to me. Two male hominids and one female hominid. Are they in the picture?"

"I don't know. Where is Sharon now?"

"Sharon?"

"The goddess of the silver screen."

"Oh. Do you know her, Julian?"

"I've met her."

"I mean, do you *know* her?"

"Not very well."

"Julian, what I mean, do you *know* her carnally?"

"I stopped answering questions like that when I was sixteen."

"Julian . . ."

"No," he said. "I don't *know* her."

Duane grinned.

"Now will you tell me where she is?"

"In her cabaña, resting. Number eight. Yeah, and listen, a truck came in about an hour ago."

"The mobile unit?"

"I guess. The driver arrived too late to catch the shuttle flight back to L.A. I put him in number twenty for the night. That's the last cabaña to the south, down by the engine house. He wants someone to sign the invoices.''

''I'll take care of it.'' He rose to his feet.

''Wait. Julian, I've got some fishermen who want to stay over for another week. Now I know that the picture people have rented everything, rooms, boats, all of it—but maybe I could put the fishermen up at my place, or back in the village. Let them use one of the boats when you don't need it. What do you think?''

''I'm not the one to talk to.''

''Maybe you could sort of sound out this Saukel.''

Julian shook his head.

''DiMotta, then, when he arrives here.''

''Duane, it seems to me that if the company rented everything, they're going to want complete use of everything.''

''I understand that. But these fishermen want to stay over. I don't care about the money, hell, I'd just charge them enough to break even. But they're hot fishermen and they have a lot of friends back in Phoenix who fish. I'd like to get them and their friends in the habit of coming here on their fishing trips instead of going down to La Paz or Cabo San Lucas or across the gulf to Mazatlán.''

''I can't help you,'' Julian said.

''Well, okay. They caught some fish, they've had fun, there's a good chance they'll come back even if I have to chase them away now.''

Julian started for the doorway, then turned. ''I'll need a boat tonight. The mobile unit's here, and DiMotta wants me to get started. I'll be gone from about 1:00 A.M. until sometime after dawn.''

"I'll fix it up. Gabaldon's the best skipper, you can have him and the big boat."

"Thanks, Duane."

"De nada."

three

Julian went down the hallway, through the restaurant, and back outside into the heat and glare. A starving yellow dog, nearly bald with mange, slept panting in the sun-ribbed shade of a palm. The glittering sea was empty except for the sudden upthrust of the island five miles offshore. It looked like a huge medieval castle from here, high-walled, with turrets and battlements and towers. An abandoned castle, crumbling now, a ruined fortress.

There was a feeling of desolation in this place, of exile, as if he had somehow been transported to the past, or into a future following the cataclysm—he could imagine himself to be the last of the race.

The resort—everyone preferred to call it a "fishing camp"—was located about halfway down the Baja California peninsula on the Sea of Cortez side. It was a barren coast; you could walk for two days in any direction before reaching anything that could be called a community. The resort was not easily accessible: There was a rough dirt airstrip out on the desert (near the small sun-struck village where the Mexican employees and their families lived); and a rutted desert and mountain road led forty-five miles to the transpeninsular highway; and of course the place could be reached from the sea. Still, it was located in an arid wilderness, and the sea and the surrounding country evoked a mood similar to that which interested DiMotta, his "abstract horror of vacuity."

Julian walked through the shadows of the orchard to the southernmost cabaña. It was the worst of the lot, unprotected from the sun, less than fifty yards from the noisy engine shed, and needing paint and new roof tiles. A white truck, the mobile unit, was parked alongside the building. The hood was up, and a short, bald man with thick hairy arms and a hairy, sunburned back was looking down at the motor.

"Trouble?" Julian asked.

The man turned. "It was cutting out a little during the last few miles. Dirty plugs, maybe."

"How was the trip down?"

"Please don't ask." He plucked a dirty rag from the back pocket of his trousers and wiped his hands. "The road in from the highway—desert, sand, potholes, ruts, mountains, cliffs . . . Three times I almost drove off a cliff. I don't know how I made it through."

"Is the equipment all right?"

He shrugged.

"Does the air conditioning work in your cottage?"

"It's the only thing that does. The lights flicker, the

toilet overflows, I got mice, no Yogi would sleep on that bed. But, yeah, the air conditioning works.''

"We'll unload the film into your cottage. This heat won't do it any good.''

They walked around to the rear of the truck, and the driver broke the seal, unlocked and lowered the steel bars, and pulled the doors open. Julian climbed inside. It was very hot. There was a smell of hot metal and gasoline. He began removing the padded tarps. Everything had been well secured and cushioned; he could not see that any damage had been done during the long trip down from Los Angeles. There were the four cameras he had asked for; a big 35mm studio camera; a smaller Bell and Howell 35mm; a lightweight 35mm Arriflex field camera; and a 16mm camera enclosed in a watertight case for undersea photography. And tripods; a stack of wooden rails that could be assembled for dolly shots; klieg lights and reflectors; mikes; hundreds of yards of electrical wire; a sound console; acoustical materials; extra lenses and filters; incident-light meters and reflected-light meters and two chromatic meters; insulated boxes of raw film stock; and half a ton of odds and ends.

The driver had climbed into the truck.

"Let's inventory this stuff,'' Julian said.

"Do you want to unload *everything?*''

"No, just the film. But I want to see that everything's here and in good shape.''

"Okay. I don't know what's what, so I'll call out from the invoice and you look for it.''

It took them ninety minutes to go through the list. There were several items missing: a 50mm lens, five twelve-volt batteries, a shotgun microphone, and a video tape unit.

"I don't know anything about it,'' the driver said.

Julian amended the invoice, noting the missing pieces of equipment, then signed it. They carried the boxes of film into the cabaña and stacked them against a wall.

"When can I get a plane out of this hole?" the driver asked.

"The picture company's Cessna comes in every day at around eleven and leaves one or two hours later."

"I can't wait. It feels like I've spent a year here, and the sun hasn't gone down yet."

Julian walked back through the orchard and then cut down to the beach. The deep, floury sand stretched for a couple of miles to the north and south and then curved seaward in long promontories. Beyond the promontories the land gradually rose into steep, schisty cliffs.

He went out onto the dock. Down in the marl-fogged water some brightly colored fish were nibbling at beards of moss. All of the fishing cruisers were out. A hundred yards from shore the big steel barge—their platform for the filming—lay quietly at anchor. The *Idler* was not far away. Its companionway hatch and port lights were open for ventilation. The boat moved easily, adjusting her bows to greet the change of tide. *Idler* was to be the young man's boat in the film. She was a squat, beamy, gaff-rigged ketch of about thirty feet, and at least thirty years old too, but still sound, and salty as hell—brass and teak, a mainmast as thick as a telephone pole, galvanized iron rigging spotted here and there with balls of baggywrinkle, and a proud bowsprit. The little yacht, like the barge, had been leased for the period of filming. Callaghan had chosen to live aboard the boat rather than take one of the cabañas. He said he liked the privacy. That meant that there would be no one around to count his drinks.

Julian decided to swim out to see him. He was wearing shorts, and so all he had to do was remove his shirt and sandals. His watch was waterproof.

He hesitated a moment—sharks sometimes cruised into the harbor to scavenge the resort's garbage and the fish entrails cast into the water by the fishing boat's crews—and then he dove in. The water was not much cooler than the air. He swam about fifty yards and then jackknifed and dove, kicking all the way down to the cool thermocline.

He could feel the pressure on his ears and sinuses. He tasted salt. Then he turned and slowly rose to the surface, spitting out little silver mushroom bubbles that he could not quite catch.

He rested a moment, then swam the rest of the way and climbed the *Idler*'s accommodation ladder. The boat, with nearly five thousand pounds of ballast, barely dipped beneath his weight. He stepped to the companionway hatch and looked down into the cabin. Callaghan, sitting on the port settee berth, was roughly massaging his right foot. He glanced up at Julian.

"A merman," he said. "Just my rotten luck."

Julian descended the steep ladder into the cabin. It was surprisingly large. There was a quarter berth, settee berths with a folding swing table between them, a pair of gimbaled kerosene lanterns, a compact galley with a gimbaled two-burner stove, an ice box, a sink and salt water pump, plenty of locker space, and a small chart table. Up in the fo'c'sle there was a chain locker, a small head, a fold-down iron frame bunk, and sail lockers.

Julian sat down on the starboard berth. "Your feet smell like fried liver," he said.

"Jesus, but they itch."

"Try a fungicide."

"Thank you, doctor, but I already have. I've bought them all, but I can't get rid of this crud."

"Go barefoot for a while. Let the air at them."

"Thank you, doctor."

"Keep them dry."

"How much do I owe you, doctor?"

Julian lifted his palm. "Please, I'm a professional man and I do not discuss fees with my patients. You will have to talk to my gorgeous secretary in the outer office."

"But, doc, I only want to know how much—"

"Stop! It's indecent to mention money to your physician. Talk to my gorgeous secretary, talk to my sexy nurse, talk to my collection agency, talk to the sheriff. You sick people are all alike."

Callaghan lowered his right foot, lifted his left, and began rubbing the toes. "Ah," he said. "Ah."

"Your feet really do stink, Mick," Julian said.

"Don't they, doctor?"

"How does stinking feet affect your love life?"

"I don't make love with my feet."

"No? I thought the Irish . . ."

"I don't like potatoes, either."

"But you like the sauce."

"Yes. Do you want a drink?"

"Are you going to have one?"

"I'm going to have one at a time. There's a jug of Bacardi Añejo in the locker beneath the sink. It's smooth, golden brown, redolent of the tropics. There are dirty glasses down there, too. Ice in the chest. Ain't life grand, Julian?"

"Beats death."

"Fetch, my son."

Julian got two glasses, filled them to the brim with ice cubes and then poured rum over the top. He placed

Callaghan's glass on the table, then sat down again.

"The mobile unit's here," he said.

"Yeah?"

"Some things are missing. A 50mm lens, a shotgun mike, batteries, and the video tape unit."

"That isn't too bad," Callaghan said.

"It isn't too good."

"Think the driver stole them?"

"I don't know. The seal on the door was intact."

"He's probably got a dozen seals in his pocket."

"Well, if he's a thief, he isn't very selective."

"Right. It's just incompetence up in L.A. You know, kid, when I was young I used to think that everyone in the world was competent except me, my family, and friends. But experience has taught me that everyone is incompetent—doctors, lawyers, generals, business tycoons, political leaders, right on down to the guy who loses things in the mailroom. Callaghan's law—all men are incompetent, but some are vastly more incompetent than others."

He finished massaging his foot. Now he smelled his hands, made a face, picked up his glass—"Cheers, pal"—and drank.

"We go to work tonight," Julian said.

"Yeah?"

"I've got a boat reserved for 1:00 A.M."

"Okay, you're the hotshot cinematographer on this turkey."

"I received a letter from DiMotta. He wants us to go out and get some atmospheric footage at night."

"Hell," Callaghan said. "We could just as easily go out in the daytime and shoot through filters. Filters, underexpose the film a little . . . *voila!* It's night."

"That's sloppy, Mick, that's really sloppy."

"You don't think DiMotta would buy it?"

"No, and I won't buy it either."

He grinned. "Do you think I'm incompetent, Mr. Cinematographer?"

"No, not incompetent. You just don't take any pride in your work anymore. It's just a job to you now."

"It was always just a job to me."

"That isn't true. You were really good once. I'll never be that good."

"That is so."

"I mean it. You were good. But not anymore."

"I *was* good," he said. "I saved a lot of pictures. I made a lot of stinking pictures smell okay, pal. I told a lot of second-rate directors to fuck off. 'No,' I'd tell them. 'You can't set up this shot. No, you can't look through the viewfinder.' I wouldn't let the bad ones near me. The good ones—they'd never *ask* to look through the camera, but they would hang around. And if I liked them, I'd step back and say, 'Hey, pal, want to take a look?' I never took any shit."

"No one's giving you any now," Julian said.

"I don't see it that way."

Julian poured more rum into their glasses. "I'm not here to give you a pep talk," he said.

"Like hell."

"You can come back, Mick."

"Come back on this turkey?"

"Maybe. If not this one, then the next."

"You say this isn't a pep talk?"

Julian smiled.

"Look, get it through your head, I don't want to come back. I don't want to work anymore. I'm sixty-two years old. I'm going to retire soon, very soon. I probably won't even finish this picture. Look, for the last couple years I've been doing porn. I've worked in forests and on beaches, in warehouses and private homes. I've spent

two years photographing people sticking foreign objects
into other people's orifices. Low-budget stuff, naturally.
Clandestine. I had to be cameraman and gaffer and recordist and sometimes even grip—what do you think the
unions would say?''

Julian shook his head.

''However, it surely has made me a horny old man.''

''You've made enough money to retire on?''

''No, I've been working on a little business deal, and
it'll probably come through any day now. When it does
. . . Spain, maybe, or Portugal. Sun and sea, pal, cheap
wine, an occasional visit to the bordello—I can get five
good years out of the money. Lavish years. I won't get
any more than five out of my liver.''

''You'll be around. You've been talking about your
little business deals for as long as I've known you.''

''This one is certain, it's a score.''

''Okay.''

''But I wish you luck, lots of it. Saukel is psycho.
DiMotta's weird. Neil Warden is stoned out of his skull
most of the time. Sharon couldn't carry a grammar
school play.''

''And me?'' Julian asked.

''You, you've got a hole in your head.''

''Not any more.''

''But you did lose some skull, right?''

''A little.''

''Got a plate in your head now.''

Julian nodded.

''Is it dangerous to you?''

''Well, it probably wouldn't do me any good if someone were to beat on my head with a heavy stick.''

''But you're okay now.''

''I think so.''

''Except for the blackouts.''

Julian hesitated. "Who told you that I had black-outs?"

"You did, Julian. Don't you remember?" Callaghan laughed. "I ninety percent believe in your blackouts because I've had blackouts myself, from drinking. But there is something creepy about the way you blot out chunks of your life."

Julian finished his drink and stood up.

"Hey, don't get mad."

"I'm not mad, I'm going to take a nap."

Julian moved to the ladder, stopped and turned. "Mick, just who is this Saukel?"

"He's putting up the money for this film."

"I know that much."

"Well, he's rich as Croesus, and has a huge palace in L.A. up at the end of Jardin Canyon that was built by one of the big silent movie stars in the twenties. Saukel used to be a very reclusive guy, I've heard, almost a hermit. He just worked, that's all. And then a little more than a year ago he found out that he's got terminal cancer, and ever since then he's been throwing crazy weekend parties at his place. Now this may be bull—the cancer, I mean, not the parties. The parties are real enough. Christ, are they real! But Saukel's a spooky guy, sort of a cross between Gatsby and Dracula. He walks around the parties with that weird smile of his and asks people, 'Do you like it here? How long do you intend to stay? Does this remind you of Versailles?' I used to like Saukel okay, he was droll, he had a neat way of gigging phonies. Now . . . I know him better, and what I know I don't like."

"Is Saukel involved in making pornographic movies with DiMotta?"

"That's right."

"And you worked for them."

"Yeah, on a couple of their pictures."

"You said they did it for the money. If Saukel is so rich . . ."

"Yesterday I *suggested* that DiMotta made porn for the money. DiMotta isn't rich. I suppose Saukel does it for the kicks. Maybe he really is dying of cancer and is cutting loose before the curtain comes down."

"Where did Saukel get his money?"

"Saukel is what the newspapers like to call an 'international financier' or 'mysterious speculator.' What does that mean? If I knew exactly where he got his money, I would have been living fat and high years and years ago. Where do guys like Saukel and Vesco and Cornfeld get their millions? Tell me, pal, please. Saukel has been indicted for some kind of fraud, pyramiding, whatever that means. But the Feds haven't been able to get him into court—he's got three dozen hotshot lawyers. And he's supposed to be sick. Maybe the cancer rumor is a lie so that every time they start getting close he can go into the hospital instead of the courtroom."

"Mick, did you attend Saukel's parties?"

"Of course. I *lived* in the house, Julian. I was DiMotta's lackey. I had my own room there, I worked and got paid."

"For shooting the porn?"

"That and other things. Saukel has a huge film library. He has some things you wouldn't believe, rare prints, erotica, the classics. I worked with the collection. I was projectionist when he needed one. I helped DiMotta, taught him some things about photography— he already knew a little—and about editing. I'm not a film editor, but I can handle the Movieola and the other equipment. Yes, I was at the parties."

"Did you ever see me there?"

"All the time, Julian, all the time."

Julian went up the companionway ladder and into the brutal sunlight. The deck burned the soles of his feet. He swam ashore, picked up his shirt and sandals on the dock, and went to his cabaña.

The window air conditioner was inefficient; it vibrated, and water that smelled a little like sewage dripped from it onto the tiles. Even so it made the room seem cool in comparison to the outside air.

He slept and once again dreamed that he was exploring a dark multileveled house. He climbed twisting stairways, slowly walked down long, narrow corridors, peered into rooms where shadows gathered demonically in the corners. Now a final level, a last hallway. There were widely spaced doors on his left, a series of tall leaded windows on his right. Wind was blowing through the trees outside, and the left wall was spattered with shadow patterns of leaves and the oblong crosshatched window frames. Ahead, at the end of the hallway, there were big double doors, intricately carved with ferns and monkeys and parrots. There were polished brass hinges and doorknobs. And above the door he saw a red lightbulb. It was not burning now. He hesitated before the doors. He was simultaneously sweating and shivering, feverish and chilled. He knew that if he found the courage to open those doors, he could then confront what horrified him—his past, his future—he didn't know. Something terrible was happening inside, an outrage that he could not bear to witness. Elsewhere in the house, down on the lower levels, came the faint sound of music—dominated by the bass—and remote talk and laughter. And something else: a thin, sourceless keening. He turned away from the doors and limped down the hallway, went down some stairs, another hallway, more stairs, and then he was back among the celebrants. A woman with long black hair and carmine lips hissed at him, hissed, and clawed the air with carmine fingernails. And laughed.

four

Julian got up at twilight. He showered, dressed in slacks, a sport shirt, brown loafers, and left the cabaña. The sky was still a luminous cobalt blue in the west, but elsewhere it had turned bluish black, and a few bright stars had appeared above the horizon. It was still very hot. Heat emanated from the earth now, rather than the sky, and it smelled like iron and ashes and bitter desert plants. The tide had gone out; there was another forty feet of beach, the dock was almost entirely exposed, and much of the sandbar that paralleled the coast two hundred yards offshore was above the water's surface.

There were big tides here; the water rose and fell as much as fifteen feet during the spring highs and lows.

The restaurant was filled with sunburned, loud, half-drunk fishermen from Phoenix and Los Angeles and

Dallas. Their evening bacchanal was underway. The men fished all day and then drank and shouted and assaulted the maids and played poker through half of the night. They were mostly middle-aged, prosperous, responsible family men who left their homes for two or three weeks each year in order to get back in touch with their essential barbarism.

Callaghan was sitting alone at the bar. Julian crossed the room and sat on the next stool.

"Having fun, Mick?"

"Oh, yeah, lots. I wish I had a funny hat." He was drunk.

Julian ordered a gin and tonic.

"You're a shit, Julian," Callaghan said.

"And you're a drunk."

"I know. I finished the jug of rum, almost." He was quiet for a time, staring down at his hands; then he said, "What am I doing here? I'm a nice guy. I give dimes to winos. I pay my union dues. I salute the flag. Why am I here?"

"Let's get something to eat."

"Not hungry. Why am I here, pal? Listen to me, Julian—I was eavesdropping on the table with Saukel and his hominids and Neil Warden and Sharon Saunders, and do you know, listen, they were talking about cinema. What is cinema, Julian?"

"It's a spice you put on buttered toast. Come on, Mick, let's eat something."

"Don't push. Cinema. Listen, I can't stand people who talk about cinema. When I hear the word 'cinema' I want to draw my revolver. This picture is going to stink. It's got that college cinema society feeling."

"You'll be able to cash the checks."

"Hey, wait, why are guys like you always named Julian and Roger and Norman and Gordon? It never fails.

Officer material. God, I despise officer material."

The bartender brought Julian's drink.

"Look at that," Callaghan said. "Gin and tonic with lime. Ain't that pretty? Why can't you Julians and Normans and Rogers and Gordons and Peters and Dexters take an honest drink?"

"Are you going to get hostile, Mick?"

"Certainly. I am *already* hostile. Did you think you could come in here full of friendship and sympathy and comradeship and escape my stupendous hostility?"

"Go easy on the booze," Julian said. "We've got to go to work in about five hours."

"Look, don't preach to me. No sermons."

"I'm giving you advice, not a sermon."

"But I don't need your advice. I was operating a camera when you were still playing with your spit. Kid, I've forgotten more about photography than you'll ever know. I really am not going to enjoy taking orders from a guy who learned the trade in television."

"You can go home."

He grinned, turned on the stool, and faced Julian. He was happy; he was eager to fight.

"Mick, I'll tell you something. I didn't want you for this picture. DiMotta asked for you. I didn't fight him, because I knew how good you used to be, and I knew that you needed work. No one will hire you anymore. I'm sorry now that I didn't persuade DiMotta to get someone else."

Callaghan was grinning crookedly. Julian thought, drunks love quarrels, they need them.

Julian finished his drink and picked up his package of cigarettes off the bar.

"You're no fun at all," Callaghan said.

"I can get a good cameraman from Mexico City. Your choice, Mick. You can be on the dock at 1:00 A.M.

nated, or one of those mean, raunchy, devious old popes."

"Look, babe," Sharon said, "I'm sure this is all very profound. But remember that you're smoking that stuff and we're not. If we were smoking, we'd probably say, 'Oh, wow, yeah,' and understand. But we're not smoking."

He smiled at her.

"Now scoot. Julian and I have to talk. And take that roach with you."

"I'd just as soon hang around."

"Tut-tut," she said. "Off you go, sweetie. Don't pet strange dogs or play in mud puddles."

Warden smiled lazily, pinched the burning coal off his cigarette, dropped the stub in his shirt pocket, and stood up. He paused at the door.

"Shar, think how nice it would be—you and me in the sack."

"Forget it."

"Some day," he said.

"Neil, just go, will you? You can't even leave a room unless someone writes you an exit scene."

"I'm not *un*straight, Shar."

"I know. Bye-bye now. Send me a postcard if you ever find home."

Grinning, shaking his head, Warden left the room.

"God," Sharon said.

"He seems a little stoned."

"A little! He snorted two lines of coke before he lit the joint. God knows what he had before that."

"I just got through talking to a drunk, Mick Callaghan, and now Warden—I'm getting high on their exhalations."

"Neil's always on something. Pot, speed, coke, smack, uppers, downers, inners, outers, all-arounders. I didn't know there were so many kinds of dope until I met Neil. Stupid. He's killing his talent. Killing himself."

"Too bad."

"Well, you got my note. Now I'll tell you what it's all about."

"I didn't get a note."

"You didn't? I left one at the restaurant. Anyway, you're here. Listen, Julian, I'm damned mad at you. Do you want a drink before I kill you?"

"No. Let's go for a walk."

They walked through the orchard to the beach and then turned south. After a few minutes she paused and, holding on to Julian's arm for balance, removed her sandals. They went on. The sand was a soft golden hue in the moonlight. There was no wind, and the arching palms were like black paper cutouts against the star-flecked sky. Small waves flashed on the beach and along the outer sandbar with a green phosphorescence, sudden balls of fire that detonated soundlessly.

"Do I smell good?" Sharon asked. "I was in a perfume commercial, and they gave me some. It's called 'Vulpine.' The same company is going to put out another perfume that they'll call 'Rapine.' It's the little things like that that make me wonder if it's worthwhile to go on."

Several years ago Julian had been first cameraman on a television movie in which Sharon had played a supporting role. She was tall, in her late twenties now, always tanned, with dark blue eyes and sun-streaked hair and good facial bones. She was wry, dry, direct, and not half as tough as she liked to appear. She was a beautiful woman and she photographed well. Julian believed that if Sharon had possessed even ordinary skill as an actress, she might have become moderately famous for five years, a media queen; but she could not act, her voice had a metallic timbre, and as soon as the cameras started running, she lost most of her natural grace.

"Did I tell you that I was mad at you?" she asked.

"Several times."

"Well, aren't you going to ask why?"

"Why?"

"Because you stood me up, that's why."

Julian was silent; he could not remember asking her out.

"Aren't you going to say you're sorry?"

"I'm sorry."

She laughed. "Jesus, Campbell, this is a moonlight stroll. Don't make me write all of your dialogue."

"I'm sorry," he said again. "I must have been drunk."

"You didn't seem drunk."

"It was at Saukel's house, wasn't it?" he said, guessing. "When I asked you out?"

"No. We were together at Saukel's, and you drove me home. We had a drink at my place and you asked me—God, Julian, don't you remember any of it?"

"No."

"Oh, terrific," she said. "I really made an impression, didn't I?" Her voice had changed. She withdrew her hand from his.

"Did we make love that night, Sharon?"

She did not answer.

"Did we?"

"I think I'm going to cry," she said.

"We did, then?"

"Or vomit."

"What can I say now?"

"Or kill you. Yes, we did make love, yes, Julian, you son of a bitch, yes."

They walked in silence for a time, and then Julian said: "Listen, I've only talked about this to the doctors and to one close friend. I'll tell you so that you'll understand. You know about my car accident. I was pretty badly busted up. I had a serious head injury. Well, every now and then I have blackouts—what the doctors call fugues. Do you understand? I have no memory of certain periods of my life. The psychiatrist believes that the fugues are pyschological, emotional. The neurologist thinks that they may somehow be connected to my head injury, but he can't explain them. Both doctors are guessing. But there it is. I must have been in a fugue that night when I was with you."

She was quiet.

"Sharon, I really am sorry."

"Is that true about the fugues?"

"It is. I'm sorry that I hurt you. But most of all I'm sorry that I slept with you and can't remember a single detail of what must have been a wonderful night."

"Okay," she said. "I didn't know. Forget it." Then she laughed. "No, *don't* forget it. Look, Julian, this isn't what I wanted to talk to you about tonight, honestly it isn't. I really wanted to ask for your help, but now it's going to sound . . ."

"Go ahead."

"It's going to sound like I'm exacting payment. It isn't like that."

"I know."

"This movie means a lot to me, Julian. Important people will see me in it. It can help me. Even if the picture is bad, I'll be seen."

"What do you want me to do?"

"You know."

"No, I don't."

"God, I hate to ask this. It sounds so vain."

"You mean that I can help you with the camera."

"Yes. You know how it is. I want to look good."

"It's my job to make you look good."

"You know how you can help me—the angles, perspective, proportion, focus, the close-ups."

"You'll be beautiful," he said.

"Have you read what there is of the script?"

"Only the first few pages."

"Well, Jesus, in the story I'm sunburned, blistered, sores all over my body, half starved . . ."

"I don't think that means too much. It's just for mood, I think. DiMotta is going to improvise. We all are, I guess."

"Okay, look, just do what you can. You can help me no matter how they make me up."

They were far down the beach now. The sea blazed with reflections of the moon and with blooming phosphorescent flashes.

"DiMotta wrote me a letter and said that this might turn out to be *my* picture, that I might become the nucleus of a dark poem. Those are his words."

"He said something similar to me. He wrote me that this might turn out to be my odyssey."

"Listen, I don't want to become the nucleus of a dark poem. What does that mean? And he said that I was going to be the nightmare life-in-death. Isn't that horrible? He's going to make me some ghastly witch in his movie. The nightmare life-in-death. God! You've got to sabotage him, Julian."

"Have you seen any of DiMotta's movies?"

"Just one, his first, *La Noche Triste. The Sad Night.* It was a sad night, all right."

"No good?"

"Static. Really dull. There were long silences where you couldn't hear anything but the crackling on the sound track. He hardly ever moved the camera. It was about a rich, decadent family in Buenos Aires, and they were shown in opposition to all these vital, life-affirming peasants. Romantic as hell.

"But there was one good detail. Throughout the film the rich family's features were changed slightly, kind of coarsened. You didn't notice it too much as the movie went along, but at the end they were all apes, chimpanzees. And in the last scene the chimps sat around drinking and smoking, and there was an uncanny resemblance between each chimp and the character it was supposed to represent. Very funny. But the picture as a whole didn't make it."

"The serious film critics liked it, I've heard."

"Sure, the French especially. But you know about the French—*Cogito, ergo cogito . . . cogito.*" She stopped. "Listen, this isn't a moonlight stroll, it's the Bataan Death March. I want to rest."

They walked up the thick, dry sand above the high-tide line and sat down. The stars vibrated overhead, millions of them, trembling like wind-blown candle flames in the indigo sky. Small waves softly hissed and died on the shore.

Sharon said, "DiMotta, in his letter, told me to get tan all over, he doesn't want the marks of a bikini on my skin. I don't know what he has in mind. There's an awful lot of casual sex in that script of his. I'll strip, I'll do nude shots, I don't care about that. But no outright sex. None of that."

"Mick Callaghan told me that DiMotta has made some hardcore pornographic films."

"Yes, I know about them."

"It's true, then?"

"You bet."

"I only half believed Callaghan."

"There's a huge room on the top floor of Saukel's mansion, it used to be a ballroom, and now it's been turned into a studio. They film up there."

"Have you ever seen the studio?"

"Yes. Saukel likes to take people up there. Hey, but listen, I was never in any of their filthy movies."

"Is the studio at the end of a long hallway, and are there double doors with carvings on them?"

"You've seen those doors? Who ever heard of pornographic doors?"

"I guess I've seen them. Did you attend many of Saukel's parties?"

"Every weekend for almost two months. It was crazy, this enormous old mossy mansion, servants carrying around trays of good champagne and Beluga caviar and little bowls of cocaine—do you think I'm kidding? Hundreds of people came, the cream and scum of Los Angeles. Big name rock bands played there, jazz bands sometimes, circus performers, all kinds of lunacy. It was fun, kind of sick in some ways too, but you could avoid the sickness."

"Is that why you attended the parties? Because they were fun?"

"That was part of it, sure. But mostly I went because there were usually people there who had power in the business, actors, producers, directors, agents. Some big names showed up at Saukel's parties. I went there to have fun, to be seen, to meet people who could help me. It worked. I met DiMotta there. We talked for a few minutes, we danced once. And now here I am. And here you are, and Neil, and Callaghan—we all met DiMotta at Saukel's parties."

"I don't remember meeting DiMotta."

"Fugued-up again, huh?"

"What is DiMotta like?"

"DiMotta. Well, he's about forty-five, I suppose, very good-looking—I mean really handsome with a square face and salt and pepper hair and candy eyes. He's got a reputation as a terrific lover, a real stallion. And he's smart. He speaks English better than you or I, with only a slight accent, and he also knows Italian and Spanish and French. And, oh, he's suave and charming. Very self-assured, but with this attractive tension beneath the surface, an intensity. He's a dynamic guy."

"What is there about him that isn't perfect?"

She laughed. "Well, he cast me as the nightmare life-in-death."

"Callaghan told me that Saukel has cancer."

"I've heard that. It could be. Look how thin he is, and weak."

"I don't like him."

"Saukel? He's the quintessential dirty old man."

They were silent for a time, and then Julian leaned over and kissed her.

She pulled away.

"I don't want to do anything that might tax your memory," she said.

They stayed there for another half hour, smoking and talking, and then walked back down the beach.

f i v e

At 1:15 A.M., Julian and David Gabaldon, the captain of the most powerful of the four cabin cruisers, were standing on the end of the dock among piles of photographic equipment. The boat was tied up nearby. A double-mantle Coleman lantern burning on the end of the dock had attracted hundreds of tiny white fish that dimpled the surface of the water and carved green commas of phosphorescence in the darkness below.

"Do you want to load the boat now?" Gabaldon asked.

"No. We'll wait to see if Callaghan shows up."

The tide was coming in again now; water swirled around the dock pilings and crept up the beach. The moon was high, and the constellations had changed positions, tilting and sliding around the dome of sky. Away from shore, Julian could see the anchor lights of the barge, the little ketch, and the resort's three other cabin cruisers.

"The tide will be right for leaving in about fifteen minutes," Gabaldon said.

Julian glanced at his watch. "The drunk son of a bitch," he said.

They waited another twenty minutes, and then Julian said, "Okay, David. He's not coming. We'll try it another night."

Gabaldon helped him carry all of the equipment back to the truck. Julian was about to lock the door bars when it occurred to him that he might be able to get some useful shots of the moon and stars out on the desert. They could later be edited into the footage taken at sea. He thought that if he could get fifteen seconds of acceptable film, the night would not be totally wasted.

The Arriflex camera had three lenses mounted on a revolving turret. He selected two additional lenses and some filters, light meters, three magazines of fast film, a small slateboard and some chalk, odds and ends, and packed all of it into a rucksack. It was not too heavy. Then he picked up the Arriflex with one hand, a lightweight telescoping tripod with the other, and started walking west.

It was fairly cool now. The moon was bright enough to cast shadows and give depth to the landscape. Dogs barked at him as he passed the little village. There was only dry brush, cactus, sharp, black stones and loose, grayish soil. The soil shined dully in the moonlight as if it, like the sea, possessed a luminous quality of its own. There was just enough breeze off the distant mountains to evaporate his sweat. The air tasted faintly sour, burnt. Now the silence hummed.

He walked for almost a half hour. He mounted the

camera on the tripod, took some light readings with the meters, fitted a lens to the camera and opened the aperture all the way, and filmed the moon isolated in the sky; waited a few minutes and then filmed it again with some wispy cirrus clouds floating by. He shot several of the brighter constellations, holding for about ten seconds on each; and then he changed the lenses and filters and filmed them again. Finally he removed the camera from the tripod and panned the Milky Way from horizon to horizon, sitting on the ground and then gradually lying back until he was supine and the opposite horizon appeared upside down in the viewfinder. He hadn't felt steady, and so he repeated the shot. That one felt good. He tried the zoom lens, turning it very slowly, slowly zooming toward the stars. A wide-angle lens. On his last shot he smeared a 50mm lens with Vaseline to get a soft, misty effect.

When all of the film was exposed he smoked a cigarette, then packed everything and started back through the surrealistic terrain.

It was like walking in a dream, a mysterious but not threatening dream.

Back in his cottage, Julian sealed the tins of film and wrote a two-page letter to the laboratory people; he provided all of the necessary technical data, described the conditions, and told them what effects he wanted (rather, what he assumed DiMotta might want).

He felt good about his work. The exposed film was nothing special; DiMotta could decide that he had wasted time and money. But he had been doing what he'd been trained to do, did well, enjoyed doing. It had been a long time.

He was not tired. He got the script from the top drawer of the desk, switched on the reading lamp, sat down and turned the pages.

* * *

...*The girl remained in her berth for five days, sleeping mostly, but sometimes sitting up and talking deliriously for hours. Nothing she said made sense to the young man. Often he would climb the companionway ladder in the middle of one of her long monologues, hear her droning below deck while he made small repairs, scanned the horizon, dozed, and then later when he returned to the cabin she would still be feverishly talking. Her eyes were bright, unseeing, she gestured with her hands and writhed with the pain of her recollections. He sometimes tried to concentrate on her words, and when he did, he understood each one, but he could never fit them together into any kind of order—by the time he assigned meaning to a particular word the meaning of the previous word had vanished and a new word was forming on her lips.*

She ate and drank as much as he gave her. If he cooked a three-pound fish, she would gnaw it to the bones. A six-ounce fish seemed to satisfy her as much. It was the same with water; a quart or a cupful, it didn't matter. Her ulcers began to heal. She gained weight. And she laughed once, when he cut his finger while filleting a fish.

On the sixth day she got out of bed, came up on deck, and sat with him beneath the cockpit awning. They talked about the sea, the sky, the earth. They talked until sunset, and it seemed to him that he had never engaged in so profound a conversation; but soon afterward he could not recall a single detail. It was the same during the following days. Brilliant, penetrating conversations, an almost miraculous lifting of veils, but all significance was lost soon after it had been revealed.

Day, night, day, night. He rigged a still to extract fresh water from salt water. Her sores healed smoothly.

She gained more weight, was tanned and healthy, she smiled and called him—he could not remember what she called him.

One day, on the foredeck, he ripped off her rotting clothes and raped her. Sweaty strands of hair were pasted against her brow. He could see clouds reflected in her eyes.

After that they had sex often; in the cabin at night, on deck in the sun, in the water among weeds and sharks and eels. He always looked for the clouds in her eyes, but he never saw them again. They did not talk anymore.

One day the young man saw an object on the horizon. It looked, incredibly, like a whale leaping clear of the water. The object remained within view all that day and was still visible when he awakened the next morning. He decided that if it really was a leaping whale, it had been stopped, frozen, at that precise instant when the long, smooth length of body had risen into the air, but the flukes remained captive in the water below. The incomprehensible time system of this place could do such a thing.

Night again, the stars burned bright holes in the sky, the horizon burned.

The object was closer on the following day. He found his binoculars and twisted the little serrated wheel until the thing jumped into focus—it was a half-sunken submarine. The section forward of the conning tower was submerged; only the conning tower itself and the rust-streaked after-hull remained above the surface. And on the tower, looking across at him through an absurdly large pair of field glasses, was a man. He wore a ragged, black wool turtleneck sweater and a cap that glittered with military insignia. The man had white beard stubble on his sun-blackened face, and white hair escaped from beneath his cap. He was laughing. At first

*the young man resented the laughter, but later, without
knowing why, he began laughing too.*

The next morning . . .

Julian dropped the script in the top drawer, stood up,
and kicked the drawer shut. To hell with it. He didn't
know how to photograph this crap. He didn't know of
any sound man who could lose the meaning of words
as he recorded them. It was all nonsense.

He smoked a last cigarette and went to bed.

That night he dreamed again of the great house, its
high-ceilinged rooms, the twisting stairways and echoing
corridors, the ornately carved double doors. Wind
thumped against the windowpanes. Moonlight projected
kaleidoscopically shifting shadows of leaves and
branches against the stuccoed walls. There was no music
rising faintly from the lower levels now, in this dream,
no muted shrieks of laughter. The red light above the
doors was burning. He paused and noticed that the carvings were more detailed than he'd remembered; half
concealed among the ferns, avidly watched by monkeys
and long-plumed birds, were many copulating pairs, men
and women, men and men, animals and women . . . He
turned and looked back; the corridor narrowed and
slanted downward with perspective and ended in what
appeared to be a small black box. Retreat seemed more
hazardous than advancing. He grasped both brass doorknobs, simultaneously turned one clockwise and the
other counterclockwise, and pushed. The doors were
heavy but well balanced; the initial momentum was
enough to swing them fully open. And he heard a
woman keening, a rhythmic, pulsing high-pitched
screaming that deafened him. Silence. And his vision
was filmed over with a viscid red color, spurting and
flowing reds, and he was blinded.

"Julian? Dear boy, what are you *doing* out there?"

The voice shocked him into partial consciousness. He was not asleep now, but not wholly awake either. He saw that he was waist-deep in the warm, salty sea. He rubbed his palms together and saw cold, green flashes erupt.

"Julian, my boy, isn't it late—or early—for a swim?"

He did not know exactly who or where he was; he felt that he had been abruptly, cruelly born with the sound of that voice. His past was lost to him. He was new, and that newness created both a giddy sense of liberty and the deepest of dreads.

A soft laugh, a quick apology. "Oh, please, I am so sorry that I laughed. You see, I sleep poorly, I rise very early, and I was walking along the beach and, well, I saw you out there splashing and frolicking like . . . And I was startled. You were singing. Did you know you were singing, Julian? It surprised me, of course. But I only laughed out of confusion, Julian, not mockery, certainly not that. Oh, really, I am so sorry, I didn't mean to disturb your morning . . . ablutions."

Julian was in the sea, yes, at night below an inverted dark bowl of sky salted with stars and sheened with the setting moon; but what sea, what skies were these?

"I'll go away if you prefer."

His memory began to return then. He still felt more than half asleep, heavy-limbed and dull, but his essential past, the huge accumulations of associations and memories and reflexes—all of the things that combine to form a personality—were returning.

"Are you all right, Julian?" Saukel, greasy-voiced and whimsical.

"Yes," he lied.

"Have you been sleepwalking?"

"No," he lied again.

"Do you have a headache?"

"No." That was true.

Saukel was wearing his cream-colored suit. It seemed to glow dimly in the last of the moonlight. Behind him, Julian could see the white cubes of the cabañas scattered here and there among the shadowy trees.

"Dear boy," he said, "I know I should be angry with you for your silly theft, but I'm not. Naughty rascal, bad, bad, bad, aren't you ashamed?"

"What did I steal?"

"You know," he said. "You tease a doddery old man, that's a mean thing to do."

"When did I steal it? Tonight?"

"No, not tonight."

"When?"

"Oh, really, I do wish you'd return my property. It has . . . sentimental value. Yes." And he laughed.

"Well, if I don't know what it is, I can hardly return it to you."

"Come out of the water, sweet boy, mischievous sprite. I hate to converse at this distance, from one element to another, so to speak."

"You come here."

"Silly lad."

"I'm not a lad, a boy, or a sprite."

"Well, then, good night," Saukel said, and then he turned and started slowly up the beach.

When he was gone, Julian swam out to the *Idler*, digging hard, kicking and pulling at full strength all the way. The water around him flamed, he was immersed in cold, green fire. When he reached the ketch he grabbed the bobstay and hung from it, resting. The seed of a headache burned behind his eyes.

He slammed his fist against the bow planks, shouting,

"Callaghan, wake up you drunken bastard!"

He turned and began swimming back toward shore. His headache seemed to expand with each stroke, and by the time he reached the sand he was nearly blind with pain. It sickened him, made him nauseated and feverish, and he heard himself moaning as he stumbled up through the sand toward his rooms.

s i x

Julian opened his eyes. Sharon, wearing a bikini, was sitting on the edge of the couch, looking down at him. Her hair was sleekly wet, her eyelashes spiky. She smelled of cocoa butter.

"How did you get in here?" Julian said.

"The door wasn't locked. I rapped until my knuckles hurt and then I opened the door and peeked in. I wasn't sure what I'd find—you with one of the maids, or even two of the maids, your corpse . . . How do you feel?"

"Not too good."

Julian had seen Sharon at the restaurant when he'd taken the cans of film there for pickup by the shuttle plane's pilot. She had suggested that they breakfast together, but Julian had told her that he was sick, and had returned to his cabaña.

Now she said, "DiMotta came in an hour ago. He wants to know if you feel well enough to see him later on."

"I suppose so."

"The Mexican technicians are expected to arrive here late this afternoon. Tomorrow or the day after we'll start work. Listen, I brought you a pitcher of lemonade. Would you like some now?"

"Yes, please."

She got up, walked to the dresser, poured lemonade into a ten-ounce plastic glass, and returned.

He drank the lemonade without pausing. "Will you get me another?"

She poured out another glass, returned and sat down on the edge of the couch again, next to his legs.

"Do you have a fever?"

Julian nodded. "Fever, killer headache, nausea . . ."

"Honestly, you men are so frail."

Julian sipped the lemonade. "I suppose Mick has turned up by now."

"No, they're still looking for him. Two of the fishermen flew their airplanes over the desert, but they didn't see him."

"He'll show up."

"Duane's afraid that he might have gone swimming and drowned."

"He's on a binge. He's unable to accept the good fortune of getting this job. I'll bet you he's crawled off into a hole somewhere with three or four bottles of booze. He'll show up in a couple of days, half dead from alcohol poisoning."

"Where could he hide around here?"

"I don't know." He finished the lemonade.

"Do you want some more?"

"No. Did you have a nice swim?"

"Yes, it was lovely."

"That's a nice bikini, Sharon."

"Do you like it?"

"It's . . . stimulating."

She smiled, stood up, moved to the center of the room and slowly turned. "I'm almost thirty," she said. "But I don't look any older than twenty, do I?"

"Maybe twenty-five." He was laughing.

"You think I'm vain, don't you?"

"You *are* vain," he said.

"I don't care. My looks are all I've got."

"That isn't true. It would be sad if it was true."

"Why?"

"Beauty isn't enough. And it doesn't last."

"What does last, Julian?"

"I don't know. Rocks?"

"I know I'm not very smart."

"Sure you are," he said.

"I'm going to be beautiful for as long as I can, Julian, then maybe I'll try to be smart."

"Okay."

"People are *always* saying that beauty can't last. So what? What does last?"

"Ugliness?" Julian said.

She stared at him for a moment and then suddenly smiled. "I don't want to fight. Shall I take off my swimming suit?"

"You should, yes. Absolutely."

"You aren't too sick? . . ."

"I feel terrific," he said.

"Still, what's the point? You'd probably forget the whole thing by dusk."

"Sharon . . ."

"Ta-ta," she said. "It wouldn't be a memorable occasion." She walked to the door.

"Sharon," he said, "women like you used to be called teases."

"Still are called teases, I believe." She opened the door.

Julian threw the plastic glass at her; it bounced off the wall and sprayed ice cubes over the tile floor.

"Sex doesn't last," she said. "Bye-bye." She slammed the door behind her.

DiMotta arrived half an hour later. He knocked on the door, opened it when Julian called for him to enter, then hesitated on the threshold.

"I'm sorry to disturb you."

"It's all right."

"Miss Saunders said that you felt well enough to see me."

"Come in."

He smiled, stepped inside, and closed the door. He was not a big man, probably no more than five feet eight inches tall and one hundred and seventy pounds, but he looked bigger. He was built heavily through the shoulders and chest, and had muscular arms and thick-boned wrists. He carried most of his weight above the waist. His hair, fairly long, receding at the temples, was about evenly mixed between black and gray.

"Really, if you would rather rest."

He crossed the room. He had lively brown eyes, a long straight nose, a wide mouth, and the type of translucent skin that shows a man's beard no matter how cleanly he has shaved. He was, as Sharon had said, a good-looking man, handsome in the style of certain French and Italian actors.

Julian sat up on the couch and they shook hands. DiMotta looked directly into his eyes. His grip was firm, dry, brief.

"I thought there were a few details we could discuss."

"Of course. Sit down. Would you like a drink?"

"No, no, thank you." He moved to the far end of the room, turned, smiled again. He moved lightly, with a self-conscious grace, like a male dancer. His feet were bare. He wore flared white duck trousers and a faded denim shirt opened to below the sternum.

"There is a doctor staying here. I'm certain that he would agree to examine you."

"That isn't necessary. I'll be fine by tomorrow."

"You've had the same illness before?"

"A couple of times."

DiMotta nodded, dragged the desk chair into the center of the room, and straddled it, his arms folded over the back.

"Well," he said. "Where to begin. I understand that the mobile unit has arrived." His accent, sounding more French than Spanish, was faint.

"Yes," Julian said. "It came in yesterday, but a few items are missing. Nothing we can't do without, except maybe the video tape unit."

He dismissed the video tape unit with a flutter of his fingers. "You are a professional. I don't need to see a setup on tape before shooting it. I'm confident that you will frame every shot beautifully. I have respect for your skill, your art. You know, this is the first time that I have worked with a photographer of your caliber. I am slightly intimidated." He smiled.

Julian knew that he was pretty good at his work, but not extraordinary; DiMotta was laying on the flattery a little too thick.

"Well. Is there anything you need?"

"A new cameraman," Julian said.

"Yes, yes, unfortunate . . . Mr. Callaghan had done

such beautiful work in the past that I thought it would be worth the risk to hire him for this picture. Would you consent to giving him another chance when he reappears?''

"No. I don't want him around."

"I understand. I shall radio-telephone Mexico City this evening and see if there is a good camera operator available. But it may take time, you understand, on such short notice, and I don't wish to delay the picture—would you object to operating a camera yourself for the first few days of shooting?"

"Not at all. I'd intended to do much of the filming myself."

"Excellent. And I have some experience, I can assist with one of the cameras."

"Fine. But let's get a camera operator here as soon as possible."

"Yes!" He said the word explosively, dramatically, and then he smiled broadly. His teeth were square, white, perfect.

Julian said, "Mr. DiMotta, I—"

"Please, call me Alfredo. And I shall call you Julian."

"I'm curious—I know nothing about the budget or the shooting schedule."

"Well, my good friend Frederick Saukel has placed seven hundred and fifty thousand dollars at my disposal."

"That isn't very much."

"It's a fortune! It's more money than I've ever had for making a picture."

"Still, these days . . ."

"But, you see, I work very fast, we have a small and cruelly underpaid cast" (he smiled) "and we will spend much less money here in Mexico than we would in the

States. The weather should be fine. We won't be harassed and bled by the unions. And also, I am sure that Frederick will give me more money if that becomes necessary. An extra one or two hundred thousand dollars means very little to Frederick. He perhaps earns that much money while he sleeps at night. It's criminally absurd, naturally, that a man should earn more money in a night's sleep than the majority of the world's population could earn in several lifetimes, but . . ." He lifted his hands palms up, smiled, and raised his eyebrows, inviting Julian to share his mirth.

"The shooting schedule?" Julian asked.

"Ah, I see that you have always worked with organized, anxious men. You will learn that each day with me is a plunge into chaos. I don't adhere to a rigid schedule, Julian. When the picture is finished it is finished. How can it be any other way? We are not manufacturing a deodorant. But—but I *believe* that twenty working days should be sufficient. Yes, say a month."

"That isn't much time."

"Enough, probably."

"It will be like working in television."

"In respect to speed, yes, but not necessarily in regard to quality. It's possible to work swiftly and have good results. It's possible to work very slowly and produce a shameful picture. Consider—if we work twenty days and average four and one half minutes of final, edited film per day, we'll then have ninety minutes. A good length for a motion picture. We'll shoot fifteen or twenty feet of film for each foot that appears in the movie, of course."

Julian shook his head. "I really don't see how we can average four and one half minutes of film each day and still maintain quality. But okay. Now, listen, I don't understand your script."

He smiled. "It doesn't matter. The script is only a mood, a hint, a direction. We must be spontaneous. Each day we shall learn what occurs each day. Julian, please, you are accustomed to working in California. You are an American with all of the charming American faith in order and schedules and logic and technology. You believe that reality can be approximated through an imitation of reality's surface. You do not believe that seven hundred and fifty thousand dollars is enough money for a motion picture because in America it often costs that much to film a thirty-second television commercial. A million dollars is paid to design a corporation's logo. A logo! Fortunes are spent to survey public opinion of the label on a can of beans. It's insane, there is no room left for creation."

Julian closed his eyes. He was exhausted. His head ached. "Look, Alfredo, I only asked about the script."

"Julian, I am not being contentious, but we are not here to make a television commercial or design a label for a can of beans. We are going to make a motion picture. Great motion pictures have been made for a fraction of what we intend to spend. Very bad pictures have been made for fifteen million dollars. Do you understand what I am saying? We are hoping to create a few moments of beauty, of art. We may fail, we probably will fail, we almost certainly shall fail. But we need freedom to try.

"You elicited information about the budget and schedule. You inquired about the script. Forget all of that. Go to work each morning in a spirit of adventure, exploration, joy."

Julian opened his eyes.

"I'll take full responsibility for this picture."

"Okay."

"It will turn out well. You'll see, we'll make a fine picture. But you must relax."

"Alfredo, I'm responsible for the photography. You don't want me to relax any more than you'd want the surgeon who is working on your heart to relax."

"On the contrary, I wouldn't wish him to be tense. Now, let me ask you a few questions. Is there room to film in the sailboat's cabin, or will it be necessary to have a cutaway cabin constructed?"

"It'll be cramped, and we'll have some difficulty with light and sound—especially sound—but we can film in the cabin."

They discussed some of the technical problems they might encounter in the filming, and then DiMotta rose from his chair.

"Thank you," he said. "I'm sorry to have disturbed you while you were ill."

"It's all right."

"I was told that you had shot some film out on the desert last night. We should receive the rushes in two or three days."

"There may not be anything you'll care to use."

"One more thing, Julian. What if I should choose to film a scene with the wrong lens, decide to effect chromatic or spherical aberration, lens flares even, what if I should elect to employ an improper parallax adjustment?"

"If it's for reasons that I understand and approve, then fine."

"And if you disapprove of my reasons?"

"I'll refuse to do what you ask."

"And if I went ahead and filmed certain shots myself, those that you refused to film yourself? . . ."

"I don't know. I'd turn down a screen credit."

"Would you stay?"

"I don't know. Perhaps."

"I understand. Well, tonight at eight I'll be giving the usual welcoming speech to the cast and crew. Come to the restaurant, if you're feeling better. And afterward I'll be showing my second picture, *Sal Si Puedes. Pass If You Can* would be a rough English translation."

"I'll try to make it."

"Good. We'll be showing films every evening on the beach. Some great films, Buñuel, Bergman, Fellini, Antonioni, Godard, and some not so great films"—he smiled wryly—"DiMotta, for example."

They shook hands again and then DiMotta started for the door.

"Alfredo?"

He turned. "Yes?"

"Have we met before? At Saukel's place, maybe?"

"I saw you at Frederick's home several times, but no, I don't believe we talked." He waited a moment, then smiled, said, "Good afternoon," and left.

Julian slept and once again dreamed that he was moving slowly down the long corridor toward the carved double doors. Again wind blew through the big trees outside and cast trembling shadows on the wall. The red light above the door was burning. Julian paused, glanced at the carvings: birds and monkeys, yes, and the copulating couples on the forest floor; but now he saw death too—a man, almost wholly concealed by the foliage, was hanging by a vine; a satyr strangled a nymph; a naked woman astride a man was stabbing him in the chest while she was being stabbed in the back by another woman; skulls and bones were scattered among the ferns. Julian placed his hands on the cool brass doorknobs, twisted them and pushed. A bar of light gradually widened as the doors swung open.

He was awakened by a heavy pounding on the door,

first blows that nearly splintered the panels, and then the door flew open and DiMotta rushed into the room. He was sweating. His mouth was twisted.

"The cameras," he yelled. "Where are they?"

"What?" Julian sat up on the couch. He was half-angered, half-alarmed by this sudden intrusion.

"The cameras," DiMotta said. "The film, everything . . ."

"The film is in cabaña number twenty. The cameras are in the truck parked alongside."

DiMotta started for the door.

"Wait! The keys are in the top desk drawer."

He returned, snatched the drawer cleanly out of its slot, scattering papers and pencils and the script all over the floor. Then he got down on his hands and knees, sorted through the litter, picked up the keys, rose quickly and ran from the room.

"DiMotta . . ."

Julian heard his footfalls receding as he ran across the orchard. He was going the wrong way. A moment of silence and then he passed again, cursing as he ran.

Julian got up. Outside he could hear other people running, hear shouts in Spanish and English.

He pulled on his tennis shorts, went outside and trotted through the orchard and down to the sea. It was mid-afternoon, hot and still and bright. Some towering cumulus clouds had formed into cauliflower and mushroom shapes far out at sea.

Running men, women, and children were scattered all along the southern beach. He saw a fat woman fall, slowly get up and then continue forward in a ponderous shuffle. DiMotta, a hundred yards away, was awkwardly running with the Arriflex camera and a shoulder bag of film. And far down the beach, near the promontory, Julian could see a group of people gathered near the water's edge. They looked no bigger than flies at this distance. Above them birds were circling, a hundred birds.

He started running. He stayed close to the water's edge.

He soon tired. There was no spring in his legs. His coordination was gone, he staggered. There was not enough oxygen in the air. No, no, he could not go on. He sat down in the sand and rested for a few minutes, then got up and slowly walked toward the crowd.

The people were gathered in a large semi-circle around a form on the sand. Callaghan, of course. It had to be. He kept walking.

DiMotta was filming the fluttering, squawking flock of birds overhead.

Julian saw Sharon step away from the crowd and walk unsteadily up the beach toward a palm.

Callaghan's body lay a few feet above the sea, left there by the high tide. His bare feet, below the trouser cuffs, looked small and white and wrinkled. His shirt was just a few ribbons of fabric now, but Julian could see that his chest, arms and face had been mutilated. There were bits of seaweed tangled in his hair. There was sand in his eyes.

The woman next to Julian was murmuring softly in Spanish. He could hear latent screams in her soft droning.

DiMotta, sweating and red-faced, moving jerkily, shouted, "*Fuera, fuera!* Get the hell out of here!" And he broke through the line and approached the body, knelt on the sand and began filming the corpse.

Callaghan had been stabbed and slashed. A knife, a machete. He had been disemboweled. His hands and forearms, raised in defense at the beginning, had been cut to the white bone. He had been bled dry; all of the wounds were white, puckered, swollen and soft-looking from immersion in salt water.

Now DiMotta stood up, made some quick adjustments to the camera, and slowly panned over the faces of the crowd.

Julian turned and walked up the beach. Sharon was still sitting beneath the palm.

"Let's go," Julian said.

"I don't know if I can walk."

He helped her up, took a part of her weight.

"No, let me go. I'm going to faint, I think."

"Come on." He partly supported her weight for the first few steps, and then she was able to walk on her own.

DiMotta, behind them now, was shouting in Spanish.

"Oh, that son of a bitch," Sharon said. She smelled of vomit. "Can you imagine taking pictures of that? It's horrible, just horrible, and I am so damned sorry I came out here."

"I know."

"Everyone started running and I ran too. I didn't even know why I was running."

"Who found the body?"

"Some kids, I heard. They were digging clams and they found Callaghan. One of the kids stayed behind to keep the birds away. The *birds*, Julian! They were—if you can't trust sweet fluffy birds, who can you trust?"

And then later. "It was ghastly. Do you suppose DiMotta intends to use that in the picture?"

They separated then; Sharon went to her room, and Julian walked to the restaurant and ordered a brandy and soda. He drank it slowly, ordered another, and asked the waiter to bring him some sheets of hotel stationery and a pen.

He wrote a letter to a friend of his in Los Angeles,

Lewis Wiggens. Wiggens was in his late sixties now, retired, but for many years he had taught film courses in the Theater Arts Department at U.C.L.A. He had helped Julian many times, with his career and personal life. He knew as much about motion pictures as anyone—the films, the directors, producers, actors and actresses, technicians, the gossip and scandals. Lewis would certainly know something about DiMotta, and maybe Saukel as well.

Julian sealed, addressed, and stamped the envelope, then returned to his cabaña and slept again. When he awakened, his headache was gone.

seven

At eight o'clock he dressed in slacks, a sport shirt, and sandals, and walked toward Sharon's cabaña. The trees were filled with quarreling blackbirds. The sky was almost wholly covered with low, gray clouds now, and the air was softer, smoother against the skin. The sky and humidity promised rain, but Julian knew that such promises are frequently broken in the desert.

Sharon was wearing a white sundress with a turquoise belt and turquoise patch pockets, low-heeled white shoes, and an old-pawn silver bracelet. She had been sunburned over her tan today; her skin was coppery and oiled. She wore a pale lipstick, thinly applied, and eyeliner and bluish green eye shadow.

"Where are you going?" Julian asked. "The Beverly Hilton?"

"I felt terrible and I had to do something to feel better and so I got dressed up."

She made two gin and tonics. Sharon sat on the leather chair in the corner, and Julian stood with his back against the air conditioner.

"Callaghan is going to be buried tomorrow morning," she said.

"So soon?"

"Mexican law. A body has to be buried by sundown of the day following the day of death."

"Mick had a couple of kids from an old marriage. Have they been notified?"

"I don't know. Duane seems to be handling the whole thing. And Duane has notified La Paz, and some policemen will be sent here to investigate the murder."

"That's good."

"I just know that Saukel's crazy hominid friends killed Callaghan."

"How do you know that?"

"I just know it, that's all. Saukel's creepy chums killed Callaghan—they had to, no one else here would do such a thing."

"Listen, Sharon, just who are these hominids?"

"They were on the beach this afternoon, gawking at the body and doing everything they could to keep from laughing."

"I didn't notice them."

"You probably thought they were hyenas. They crashed one of Saukel's parties last spring. He was amused by them, I guess. He keeps them around. You've seen a lot of the type—stupid, vicious punks. The girl told me that she'd been a hooker in San Francisco for a couple of years, and God, she can't be more than twenty now. She's written to Charles Manson in prison and got letters back from him. One of the guys was a biker up in Oakland, not a Hell's Angel but in one of those gangs. He's done time. The other one says he's a shaman. It's scary when you think about how many zombies like that are walking around. Burnt out on drugs and violence and sick sex.''

"The apocalypse is near," Julian said, smiling.

"Listen, I'm not kidding. There are casualties like that everywhere these days, empty, vacant, morally dead. They scare me. I'm a little bit frightened all of the time. This is the era of the psychopath. You're smiling again—do you think I'm exaggerating?''

"A little, maybe.''

"Well, if you could be a woman in Los Angeles for about one week, you'd learn something about fear.''

They finished their drinks and left. The restaurant was crowded tonight: There were a half-dozen fishermen who would be flying out in the morning; Neil, DiMotta, Saukel and his hominids, and eight Mexicans of varying ages—the technicians and assistants. Among them would be the sound team led by the mixer, with a recordist and mike man; a gaffer and his helper, both of whom would work with Julian on the lighting; an assistant director, perhaps; a grip; a makeup man. It was not a large crew, but then this was not a big production; DiMotta was very smug about thinking small. Julian hoped that the new camera operator would arrive within a few days.

Sharon and he sat down at a table next to the front window. She ordered a vodka martini; Julian, a bottle of beer.

"This afternoon," Sharon said, "I thought that I'd never be able to eat again. Now I'm starving. So much for shock and grief.''

They both ordered gazpacho, cold German potato salad, crayfish tails, and glasses of white wine.

"Look at these faces," Sharon said. "This room is filled with the kind of people you try not to look at when you pass them on the street."

Saukel and his hominids were sitting at a table half-way across the room. The girl was tall with long, straight hair that had been bleached or stripped snow-white, and it fell over her cheeks in two wings. She had a wide, sullen mouth. Her bare feet were dirty. She wore denim coveralls.

Neither of the men wore shoes or shirts. One, a sallow boy with a sandy beard and frizzy hair, was so thin that his rib cage and shoulder blades were clearly outlined beneath the skin. He looked ill, half-starved, and he moved and spoke listlessly.

The other man was big, nearly as tall as Saukel but much heavier, with a thick, black beard and black hair tied back in a pony tail. He was older than his two friends, perhaps thirty. He sprawled lazily in his chair, insolently staring at—challenging—anyone who happened to meet his eyes. He looked at Julian contemptuously, nodded, smiled to himself. There was a tattoo on his chest with the word *MOTHER* written in a large fancy scroll entwined with flowers; and below that, in small red print, *fucker*.

"You'd probably," Sharon said quietly, "find blood mixed in the dirt beneath their fingernails."

"I have no intention of looking under their fingernails," Julian said.

DiMotta was eating alone at a table beneath the stuffed marlin. Every now and then he set aside his fork and jotted a few lines in a leather-bound notebook.

The Mexicans, all sitting together at a long table, were chattering noisily and cheerfully in Spanish.

Now DiMotta closed his notebook, picked up his fork,

and tapped it against a water glass. The room gradually became quiet. DiMotta rose to his feet.

"I had intended to make the usual director's speech," he said, "welcome all of you, introduce you to each other, explain our goals. . . . Never mind that.

"You know about Mr. Callaghan's . . . death. I almost said 'tragic death,' but that would have been false, a hypocrisy. One does not have to be an Aristotelian to know that for tragedy to exist there must be a hero. And those of you who knew Mr. Callaghan must agree that there was nothing heroic in his nature.

"Still, he was a man, and he is dead, and it is customary to make a gesture on these occasions. There will be services at the village church at nine; interment at ten or ten-thirty. Perhaps you will choose to attend.

"Each night we'll be showing films on the beach, and the daily rushes when they begin arriving. Tonight the feature will be *Sal Si Puedes*—my second film. If any of you have a special request, a movie that you've always wanted to see, or wish to see again, please let me know."

He paused, then went on: "I would like to suggest that all of us will enjoy the next month or so, but I can't. I suspect that you'll be miserable. I hope to utilize your rage, your self-pity, your weaknesses." He sat down and opened his notebook.

Saukel had been whispering during DiMotta's speech, and now, in the continuing silence, the girl with him said, "Oh, you can't get it up anymore and so you like to watch other people do it."

The two men laughed.

"Outrageous!" Saukel hissed.

"Well, isn't it so?"

"Impotence is a *virtue* at my age." He picked up his Panama hat and the walking stick and slowly, stiffly, stood up. He appeared to be furious. He glowered at them for ten or fifteen seconds while they grinned, and then he rapped his cane on the floor. The steel ferule left tiny triangular holes in the wood.

"Ungrateful waifs," he cried.

They laughed at him.

Saukel, skeletal and trembling, tapped his cane on the floor three more times. He looked old and sick and vulnerable, a severely offended old gentleman. "Refuse of the industrial society!" he said. "Scum." His voice cracked. "Sewage of democracy!"

"Oh, sit down, Freddy," the girl said.

Everyone in the room was watching them.

"Fecal matter!" Saukel yelled, still trembling and beginning to weep now. "Products of your mother's bowels."

And then he turned and stalked across the room and out the door. As he passed, Julian saw that his lips were turned up impishly at the corners, and his eyes, lensed with tears, were bright and happy.

"I can't believe it," Sharon said. "What a zoo."

"Saukel was clowning."

"So what? It's still a zoo."

"Excuse me," Julian said, and he left the table.

Saukel was about thirty feet ahead of him, walking slowly toward the sea.

"Saukel," Julian said. "I'd like to talk to you."

He turned. "Why, Julian, how generous to want to speak to a futile, senile, disgraced old man."

He waited until Julian reached his side, and then they walked down to the water's edge and then turned north.

"Ah, lovely," Saukel said, pointing with his cane. "Look at that seashell, see the delicate rainbow hues shimmering in the glossy pearl, see the way it fans out, the serrations—it's a petrified baby angel's wing, no doubt. Julian! The Lord is safely ensconced on His throne!''

''That was a fine performance in the restaurant.''

''Beastly youths,'' he said. ''They're not even clean. One has a right to expect youthful cleanliness from youth, at least that.''

''Why do you keep them around?''

He shrugged. ''They're smarter than cats and dumber than dogs. And they don't soil the carpets.''

''You seem to know me, Saukel, but I don't know you.''

''Ah, Julian, there is something sweet about you.''

''No, there isn't.''

''You are right! There isn't. You caught me there.'' He laughed. ''I lie, yes, you know that, I do lie. I'm much too old to tell the truth.''

''How old are you?''

''Ninety-eight.''

''Crap.''

''You caught me lying again! Well, gee whiz, what can I say?'' The 'gee whiz' pleased him; he smirked, lengthening his long jaw and enclosing his eyes in webs of wrinkles.

''What did I steal from you?''

''A dream. Julian, lad—do you mind?—I am not well, already tired. I would like to rest.'' Slowly, using his cane for support, he lowered himself to the sand. ''Ahhh.''

''I attended some of your parties.''

''Yes.''

''But I don't remember them.''

''I understand. I understand that now. Your accident.''

''I talked to you about my loss of memory?''

''Once, briefly.'' Saukel withdrew a cigar from an inside jacket pocket, unwrapped the cellophane, neatly bit a hole in the tip, and said, "Dear boy, do you have a match?"

"Yes," Julian said.

"Then will you strike one and light this cigar for me?"

"No."

"*No?* Where has civility gone? I'll give you one hundred dollars if you'll light this cigar."

"You have a large upstairs room in your house, a studio where you and DiMotta make pornographic movies."

"Nonsense."

"I dream about that room."

"Sir, I am not responsible for your architectural and erotic dreams."

"What did I steal from you, Saukel?"

"Listen, my boy, I'll give you five hundred dollars if you'll light my cigar. That is no joke. I'll write you a check immediately or I can get the cash from the hotel safe when we return."

"No," Julian said.

"But it's such a simple act, courteous—strike a match, lean over, and apply the flame to the end of my cigar."

"No."

"Please."

Julian shook his head.

"Why *not?*"

"I'm not one of your hominids."

"You are not a five-hundred-dollar hominid, at any rate."

"You refuse to talk seriously to me, then?"

"Oh, Julian, honey, I will talk seriously with you when *you* are ready—able—to discuss certain sensitive matters."

Julian turned and started back toward the restaurant.

"Julian, it's all right," Saukel called. "I do not judge you." He laughed. "Who am I to judge?"

Sharon was halfway through her meal when Julian sat down at the table.

"Thanks a lot for leaving me here," she said. "I enjoy eating alone."

"I'm sorry, Sharon. It was important."

"What could be important about talking to that warlock?"

"I'll tell you about it later."

She shrugged. "First you eat, then you talk." And then: "At least the gazpacho and the potato salad are supposed to be eaten cold."

"Rock lobster tail is good cold too."

"You're so amiable. I hate that."

Julian had finished eating and was on his second glass of wine when DiMotta closed his notebook, got up, and walked toward their table. He was wearing faded Levi's and a striped French fisherman's shirt. There was a single strand of black coral beads around his neck.

"May I join you for a moment?" he asked.

Julian gestured toward an empty chair.

He sat down. "Good evening, Sharon."

"Ghoul evening, Alfredo."

He smiled at her.

Sharon, exhaling smoke, looked at him through half-lidded eyes. "I don't think it was cool of you to use the camera this afternoon, Alfredo. It was very uncool, in fact."

DiMotta, still smiling, nodded. "Cool, uncool . . . Well, perhaps you are right. In fact you *are* right—it was uncool of me to use the camera. I admit it. And I don't care. I am not terribly interested in convention, you see, in coolness. I was callous this afternoon, true. Fevered."

"Tasteless."

"I am not concerned with taste."

"You ought to be."

"I am concerned with art."

"So is taste," Sharon said.

"Is it really?" DiMotta said. "Think about it."

He signaled the waiter and asked him to bring a round of drinks to the table.

"I have been making notes for a motion picture I would very much like to make," DiMotta said. "I was walking on the desert late this afternoon. The heat was terrible. Cactus, withered brush, scorched black stones. I wandered around out there and I thought, yes, perhaps this is the place to make my Vietnam movie."

"Yes?" Sharon said.

"You are thinking, a Vietnam movie shot on the desert? What about the rain forests, the rivers and rice paddies, the mountain wilderness? But don't you see, the desert would provide the perfect spiritual analogue to war. Desolation, blasted earth, sterility. There are many Vietnamese exiles living in California. I could bring some of them here."

"I'll bet they would recognize your spiritual analogue immediately," Sharon said.

DiMotta smiled faintly and nodded, as if approving of her cleverness.

"Honestly, Alfredo, I don't know which is worse, your photographing Callaghan's corpse this afternoon or your ugly, stone-hearted references to him this evening."

"What do you mean?"

"That 'nothing herioc in his nature' stuff."

"Perhaps I should have said that right now Michael Callaghan is a star in heaven."

"You could have mentioned the services and dropped the rest."

"Or perhaps I could have stated that all of us, every one, has been diminished by Callaghan's death. The bell has tolled for thee."

"You should have shut your mouth, then and now."

"I know, I know, do not speak ill of the dead. If you can't say anything nice about a person, then say nothing at all. And so forth. Right? Callaghan was a weak man, so weak that he could not preserve his modest niche in the world. I mean professionally, personally, socially and—finally—physically."

"But, my God, it's freaky to hate him because he was weak!"

"I didn't and don't hate him. Of course not. How can one either love or hate a Callaghan? The Callaghans of this world are beyond love and hate."

"All human life is precious."

DiMotta smiled. "Your platitudes, Sharon, are uglier than my stone-hearted assertions. Callaghan was ordinary, common, a weed. By definition what is common cannot be precious. Only the rare is precious, the rare mineral or gemstone, the rare work of conquest or genius. But Callaghan? The world is a very bearish market for humanity such as Callaghan."

"And for me too, then," Sharon said. "I'm a weed."

"Perhaps so. But it remains true that the human race succeeds because of its exceptional members, not its exceptional numbers. Really, what is one sardine to the oceans, one Callaghan to the earth?"

"Or one DiMotta."

"Indeed, or one DiMotta, if I lack will. That's the determining factor, strength of will, triumphal will." He smiled at Sharon, nodded to Julian, then rose and left the room.

Sharon sat quietly for a time and then said, "Julian, what was he talking about?"

"Biology, I think."

eight

It was almost dark when they went outside. Workmen were setting up the screen and projector on the beach. Most of the people of the village were there, sitting or lying on blankets, talking excitedly. This was a special occasion for them; a movie, and free at that.

Julian and Sharon sat down next to Neil Warden. He was staring intently at the blank screen.

"Hello, Neil," Sharon said.

"Shhh," he hissed.

"Very funny."

He whispered: "We are privileged to view Alfredo DiMotta's famous *ex nihilo nihil fit* scene."

"What does that mean?"

"Out of nothing, nothing comes."

Sharon looked at the screen. "Yeah. White on white. It must be one of his analogues."

"No, this is a metaphor."

She looked at him. "What kind of dope are you on tonight, Warden?"

"None. Zero. I'm off drugs. They're rotting my brain."

"I'm glad to hear it. I'll be even gladder to believe it. Have you seen this movie *Sal Si Puedes*?"

"Yes."

"Is it any good?"

"Well, that depends on your viewpoint. Do you like home movies?"

"No."

"Juliano?"

"No."

"Well, there you are. I love home movies. Ma and Pa squinting into sunlight, baby with his dirty diapers, everything off-speed, ghastly shadows crawling off the screen toward you . . ."

"That bad, huh?"

"No, actually I like the story very much. But technically . . ."

A cone of light leaped across the darkness and illuminated the screen.

SAL SI PUEDES

The sound of drums and flutes and, in the background, automobile traffic. And then a blurry image—quickly brought into focus by the projectionist—of a pretty young woman hurrying down a crowded market street. She pauses every now and then to look at the objects being sold, melons, oranges, bright bouquets of flowers, live birds, fish on ice, and then she goes on again, smiling happily to herself.

The credits are superimposed on the scene. More drums are playing now, and more flutes, and in the background the sound of automobile horns and the cries of vendors. The woman pauses to look at her reflection in a store window; she wipes away an errant fleck of lipstick with her little finger, lightly touches her hair.

Cut to a dark, brutal-looking man in a battered open sports car. He drives slowly along the street, stops when the woman stops, drives slowly on when she moves.

POR
ALFREDO DIMOTTA

The woman sees the man and his car reflected in the window glass; she frowns, turns sharply, and resumes walking down the crowded sidewalk. More drums and flutes now, playing louder in a kind of bolero.

"God, I love movies!" Sharon whispered.

"Too bad the movies don't love you, Shar," Neil said.

Insects and bats flew through the bright cone of light and were briefly magnified into shadow monsters—moths as big as hawks, bats as big as eagles.

Julian lit a cigarette and watched the movie. He was primarily interested in the photography. It was not good. Cheap film, poor lighting, careless set-ups. The colors were mostly gaudy comic-book reds and blues; all the subtler rays of the spectrum were overwhelmed.

Sharon had said that the camera had not moved enough in *La Noche Triste*; but in this picture it moved too much and without design, rapidly changing angles and focus, panning excessively, and employing many unnecessary tracking shots. The photography was bad.

Worse, it was vulgar; there was no rhythm, no sense of pace. The cameraman had been incompetent. The director—DiMotta—had been unsure. The editor—DiMotta again—had made a technically bad picture worse. A good film editor might have pieced the hundreds of diverse shots together in such a way as to have created a unified whole. The puzzle could have been assembled differently and improved.

Halfway through the picture Julian leaned close to Sharon and invited her to the restaurant for a drink.

"What?" she whispered. "*Why*?"

"I can't stand any more of this."

"Another snotty citizen," Neil said. "Votes with his feet."

"It isn't bad at all," Sharon said. "I like it. The girl is very good."

Now the brutal-looking man and the young girl were eating lunch on a terrace that overlooked a neon-purple ocean. "*Verdad?*" the girl said, and a subtitle at the base of the screen read: "Is it true?"

"Don't you like the story?" Sharon asked.

"I haven't been paying much attention, but from what—now, look at that, a goddamned lens flare."

"Be quiet," Sharon said.

"Down in front!" Neil shouted.

"Oh, God," Sharon said softly. "Please shut up, Neil. Julian, watch the movie. Follow the story, forget all the technical crap."

"I can't take these colors," Julian said. "And the jump-cutting is giving me tics."

"*Y entonces*?" the brutal-looking man was saying. The subtitle: "And then?"

The girl said that she was going away.

The camera abruptly changed angles and from a close-

up to a medium shot, and for an instant the figures were
outlined in pale violet.

"Shit," Julian said, and he got up.

That night he dreamed that he was running up long,
steep stairways and down endless dark halls. Tired, he
was so tired. Now down the last corridor. It seemed
miles long and narrowed to a thin rectangle of light. He
went in through the open doors. Bright lights, ululating
screams, glottal shrieks, shrill keenings. Giants were dying before him, writhing giants with twisted mouths,
glazed eyes, blood everywhere, screaming, knives falling, rising, falling again, blood spurting. Monsters with
human bodies and animal heads, wolves, reptiles, hyenas, birds of prey.

He had been too slow, too late, much too late. The
two women had died. Were still dying somehow, over
and over again, and would continue to die for a long
time, years perhaps.

He closed the doors, pulled them hard until the locks
clicked, and then he turned and walked down the hall.
His heels made reports like small caliber gunfire on the
tiles. He swung his arms. He whistled a tune as he
walked. From below he heard music and voices and
laughter. This was not a bad party. Downstairs there
were attractive women and good food and drink and
music. All the ingredients of an adventure. First, though,
he would wash the blood off himself. Then a bite to eat,
a stiff drink, and after that . . . who knew?

The woman with the carmine lips and fingernails was
standing at the base of the stairway. She hissed at Julian
and clawed the air. The girl with her, a small blonde
with a cast in one eye, laughed and said, "No, he's not
the one." They were the two he had seen murdered (and

were still being murdered) in the room upstairs.

They had not been masked. They had been killed (were still being killed, would always be killed, over and over again) by predatory animals with human bodies.

nine

Early the next morning Duane flew down to Santa Rosalia and returned two hours later with a young priest. Services were held in the little adobe church in the village; Callaghan was then buried in the cemetery several hundred feet out on the desert. All of the movie people and many of the villagers attended the ceremonies. None of Mick Callaghan's relatives were present, probably because there had not been time enough to make the rather difficult travel arrangements, Julian thought.

Julian and DiMotta walked back to the resort together. It was almost noon; the sun was high, the shadows compressed, and they both sweated in their dark suits. A hot bitter-smelling wind blew down from the mountains. Ahead and to their left, Duane and Neil and Sharon walked together, talking quietly. And behind them, Saukel—who had been pious and somber all morning, like a well-paid mortician or professional mourner—limped along with his cane. Others, movie people and employees of the resort, were scattered over the empty terrain, moving slowly toward the cool, green orchards.

"You were Callaghan's friend . . ." DiMotta said.

"I knew him a long time," Julian said.

"I don't suppose you'd be willing to work today."

"I'll work."

"I'd like to have everything set up for tomorrow morning. Have you considered about how we might be able to shoot the sailboat scenes?"

"Why not take the sailboat and the barge out to the island. We can shoot with the island at our back, looking toward the open sea."

"That was my thought. But isn't the water in the shallows around the island a different color?"

"Yes, but it shelves off rapidly. We can anchor the sailboat on the edge of the reef and shoot past it into blue water."

"Good. You can photograph from the barge, and I'll try to get some additional footage from one of the cabin cruisers."

They entered the orchard. The air was cooler here, moister and sweeter.

"Preparations are being made now," DiMotta said. He glanced at his watch. "Why don't you meet me on the dock at one?"

"Fine."

"I appreciate your willingness to work today, on a Sunday, and after the funeral."

"There's not much else to do around here except work."

The island was only five miles offshore, but they had to move slowly to prevent the engines of the two tow boats from overheating. It took them an hour to reach the island and another hour to get the sailboat and barge securely anchored. They would remain there for at least two weeks, DiMotta said, and so they had to be certain that the anchors were properly set, with plenty of scope and clearance enough to compensate for changes of wind and tide. An armed watchman would remain with the boats and equipment at night.

Then DiMotta and Julian sat on the barge, in the shade of a big awning the workmen had erected. One of the cabin cruisers had returned to the resort, and the other waited for them.

"Yes," DiMotta said. "I think this will do."

The barge was anchored about one hundred yards away from the northern tip of the island. The sailboat had been positioned another seventy-five yards north of the barge. The barge would have to be moved each morning for the filming. Behind them, in the shallows, the water was an intricate mosaic of color, lime green and turquoise and pale milky greens, gradually darkening as the reef shelved, to indigo and cobalt blues. The water was clear; looking down, Julian could see the jagged submarine architecture of the reef sixty feet below, and swaying purple sea fans, clumps of spiky grass, and scattered patches of snow-white sand.

"What did you think of *Sal Si Puedes*?" DiMotta asked.

"I didn't see all of it."

"I know. I saw you leave."

"It was technically bad."

"It could have been better that way, yes."

"The camera work, lighting, sound, lab work—and where the hell did you buy that film stock? It looked like something left over from 1939."

DiMotta smiled unhappily, nodded. "I did all that I

could on a very limited budget. But now, thanks to Frederick, I can afford to buy high quality film, employ the facilities of a good laboratory, hire a professional crew."

"Well, you know what I think of your budget for this picture, and how fast you intend to make it. Who was your cameraman?"

"I am responsible for most of the photography," he said. "Ninety percent of what you saw last night was my camera work."

Julian laughed briefly. "Well . . ."

DiMotta was silent for a time, and then he said: "You know, don't you, that my pictures have been very well received in Latin America and Europe. And from certain critics in the United States."

"I've heard that. But I've only been talking about technical matters."

"The *science* of filmmaking," he said contemptuously.

"That's right. That's my province."

"Well, I advise you to remain within your province."

"That's what I've been trying to do."

"There is also the *art* of filmmaking."

"I know. Look, talk to Sharon, she liked your picture. So did most of the other people who saw it last night."

DiMotta got a package of cigarettes from his shirt pocket, offered Julian one and took one for himself.

"Are Sharon and Neil to be the entire cast?" Julian asked.

"No, probably not. I think I shall use Frederick also."

"Saukel? He's not an actor."

"Of course he is. Everyone is an actor, and Frederick far more than most. He is acting all of the time, as you surely must have noticed. There is something brilliant in Frederick's creation of his persona. Persona, Julian, is a

Latin word whose original meaning referred to the masks worn by actors.''

''I know.''

''I shall probably use Frederick's amusing persona in this film, encourage him to play himself playing himself.''

''Any others?''

''I can't say now. I might use Frederick's young savages. And I might ask some of the villagers to appear in the picture, or even you, Julian. Or it could be that a stranger will appear here just when I need him, when he offers himself as the solution to a problem that did not exist before his arrival.''

Julian nodded, defeated by another of DiMotta's semi-mystical pronouncements.

''Have you explored the island?'' DiMotta asked.

''Some. There's not much there. A few beaches, a cave on the gulf side, a fairly large plateau that slants up toward the summit.''

''Could we move the equipment around up there?''

''Yes, but it would be a lot of work.''

He nodded, looking over Julian's shoulder at the island. ''The thing attacks the spirit,'' he said. ''A fragment of a dead star. Is there any life?''

''Birds, lots of birds. And there are lizards, and maybe some snakes. I didn't see any snakes.''

''Mammals?''

''Rats, probably.''

''Nothing larger?''

''I doubt it.''

''No feral goats or pigs?''

''No.''

''Well, we can bring our own goats and pigs. Our mariners must reach land eventually. That is the perfect place. A land as harsh and uncompromising as the sea.

We shall learn if our poor lost ones make any mistakes up there. Nature, you know, does not tolerate error. Tonight you must sketch the island for me.''

"I took about one hundred and fifty Polaroid shots."

"You did? Wonderful."

"They're in my room. I'll give them to you when we get back."

He smiled. "I can see that I'm working with professionals this time."

"Except for Saukel," Julian said.

"I want starkness, cold, plastic forms, desolation, a devouring sun. Yes, I like that monumental cinder. Julian, I am interested in life on the abyss, the deprivation that leads to a madness that spirals back inside of itself to a deeper reality."

"Yes?" Julian said.

''We know nothing about people, nothing, until we have seen them attempt to function under extreme duress, pushed to their limits and beyond. Our friends, lovers, neighbors—they are lies, poorly constructed lies. As history is a lie. History is the lie of attributing rational human motives to irrational crimes. Our concept of humanity is the result of many thousands of years of deceit and terror. We lie because we cannot bear the dread that accompanies truth. Do you see? But the dread still exists within us, there is dread in our laughter, our sex, our isolation, our dreams. Ah, but what do you do when the lies are no longer tenable, when the lies will inevitably lead to more agony, increased suffering, even death?"

He smiled and slowly shook his head. "Then you will see the true nature of the race, stripped of hypocrisy, of all of the lies we've peddled to each other to repel the dread. I am talking about survival now. War, famine, disaster, anarchy . . . I am talking about psychic revolution, upheavals of the soul. When man finds society's codes and values irrelevant to the situation, he will revolt and assert his true nature. And he will know—perhaps exultation?''

''I'm not sure I understand what you mean,'' Julian said.

''I am talking about the process by which dread is converted into exultation. I am talking about what happens when we are suddenly freed from society's restraints, the civil laws outside of us, and the moral laws internalized within us. I am talking about how people behave during war, famine, crisis.''

''Some people behave very well,'' Julian said.

''I am telling you that we are all cannibals. If there is enough stress, enough hardship, enough deprivation, the dread turns into exultation, and we become the most ferocious beast on the planet. Conscience is the name we give our weakness. Morality is a euphemism for cowardice. In each of us there is a murderer, a torturer, a cannibal.''

Julian smiled faintly. ''We'd better go in now,'' he said. ''This sea air stimulates the appetite.''

DiMotta laughed.

t e n

The first week's shooting went well enough; DiMotta was confident that he would meet his quota of four and one half minutes of usable film per day after editing. They shot much more than that, of course. They worked hard for brief periods, waited, set up a shot, waited, filmed, waited some more. Making a motion picture was a lot like fighting a war, Julian thought; there were long stretches of boredom interspersed with sudden flurries of action.

The crew was small that first week; they had no need for artificial lighting, no scenes containing dialogue, and so the electricians and sound men were not on call. Background noises—the sounds of the sea, the creaking and groaning of the sailboat's hull and gear—would be dubbed in later.

They usually ate breakfast at five-thirty and by six o'clock were on their way out to the island. It was fairly cool then, and the light was superb; the colors were purest between six-thirty and eleven. After that Julian had to make a great many calculations concerning the film stock, filters, lens aperture, etc., in order to compensate for the fading colors and the harsh reflections.

They filmed Neil alone on the deck of the *Idler*: he posed leaning against the mainmast, pretending to take sights with a sextant; he lay supine on the foredeck; he dozed beneath the cockpit awning; he moved slowly, displaying "heat-drugged indifference" as he submitted to "timeless time and unintelligible space." And they took some long shots of Sharon alone on a yellow life raft, and then more shots of her with Neil on the deck of the sailboat.

Julian worked on the barge while DiMotta, aboard one of the cabin cruisers, offered suggestions to him and the actors through a battery-powered megaphone. And sometimes he filmed with the Arriflex field camera, shooting at the same time as Julian, but from a different angle and distance.

They usually returned to the resort in mid-afternoon when the sun-glare spoiled photography. The afternoon and evening hours were tedious, repetitive; they went to their cottages and showered and napped, ate dinner at dusk, and then watched the rushes from the previous day's shooting and a movie that DiMotta had selected—often boring—and then they slept, and, too soon, it was time to get up and return to work.

Julian borrowed a face mask, fins and a snorkel, and when he had a few minutes to spare he dropped over the side of the barge and dived. Fish darted into the cracks of the reef as he approached. Silver barracuda, poised like arrows, curiously watched him. Sea grasses swayed plastically with the currents. Objects were magnified, sound amplified—footsteps up on the barge reverberated like thunder. The scattered moments that he spent diving were always the best parts of his day.

At noon he usually swam over to the *Idler* and joined Sharon and Neil for lunch. They sat in the shade of the cockpit awning and ate sandwiches and drank cold cans of beer. They both had been burned over their tans, and their hair had been dried and burnished by the sun.

On Friday, Sharon said, "Well, what do you think of this picture so far?"

Julian shrugged. "It doesn't seem to be going anywhere."

"Precisely. According to Mr. D., by tonight he'll have approximately twenty-two minutes of film, a third of the picture. And of what? Nothing. Twenty-two minutes without a word of dialogue, without the merest hint of a plot. All of these five- and ten-second shots—it's going to be a series of five hundred non sequiturs."

"I suppose," Julian said, chewing.

"The three rushes we've seen so far look good," Neil said.

"Sure," Sharon said. "The photography is terrific. Julian's photography is—DiMotta's stuff isn't much."

Julian opened a can of beer. "DiMotta promised me a cameraman. He hasn't showed yet. I don't think he will."

"Listen," Neil said, "do you know what DiMotta suggested to me? He thought it would be a great idea if we caught a bunch of fish and gutted them and let them bleed into the water to attract sharks. Okay? And then I was to go swimming over the side—like in his script."

Sharon laughed.

"He said they could rig some kind of harness and snatch me out of the water if any sharks got aggressive.

And so there I am, swimming in fish guts and blood—he'd love to see me eaten by sharks. Good publicity."

"Yeah," Sharon said. "He could maybe superimpose you being eaten by sharks over views of Callaghan's corpse."

"DiMotta is . . . unique," Julian said.

"Sáukel is . . . unique," Sharon said.

"But they're both superbright guys," Neil said. "You've got to admit that."

"Listen, Julian," Sharon said, "DiMotta wants me and Neil to screw for the cameras. Did you know that?"

"No."

"He wants us to get into all kinds of heavy sex, all over the boat, in the cabin, the water—halfway up the mizzenmast too, I wouldn't doubt."

"I thought it was a good idea," Neil said, looking at her.

"I think the idea of you swimming with the sharks is even better."

Julian opened another can of beer. "What did you tell him, Sharon?"

"I said, 'Look, Alfredo, are you making this picture for Sleazy-Sam's porno parlor? If you are, I'll go home now.' "

"That isn't what you said," Neil told her.

"It's close to what I said."

"There's a lot of money in porn," Neil said. "That's where a lot of the new fortunes are being made, porn and dope."

"DiMotta," Sharon said, "talked about art. Naturally. He said that movies could explore sexuality with the same honesty as modern literature does. Sex is the last human frontier, he says. Film is waiting for its Joyce, its D. H. Lawrence. There are entire realms of carnality that haven't yet been explored. God!"

"DiMotta doesn't mention his plans to me," Julian said. "I'm only his director of photography. Does he still intend to bring in the German submarine captain?"

Neil shook his head.

"Something better," Sharon said.

"What's that?"

"You won't believe it," Neil said to Julian.

"Death," Sharon said.

They were grinning.

Sharon brushed the hair away from her eyes. "Saukel is going to appear in the picture. As death. Mr. Death."

"He'll greet us when we land on the island," Neil said.

"Saukel playing death. Can you imagine?"

"Typecasting," Julian said.

"And Saukel's degenerate hominids are going to appear in the picture too. I don't know as whom. Or what."

Julian got another sandwich from the cooler and removed the wax paper wrapping. "Maybe as Pestilence and Famine and War," he said.

Sharon laughed. "I just don't care anymore. This picture will never find a distributor. Well, okay, as long as they keep issuing the checks."

"Shar," Neil said. "Next week we get naked."

"I'll do a nude scene or two," Sharon said. "I don't like the idea much, but I'll go along. But that's all. No sex and that's it—no porn."

Neil grinned. "You've got a stand-in for the serious porn."

"What? No, you're kidding. Who?"

"The female hominid, Cally."

"Oh, Neil, you're kidding."

"Nope."

"That pig!"

"Is this true?" Julian asked.

"It is," Neil said. "And so one of these days you'll have to shoot some close-ups of Sharon when she's affecting great passion. I'd guess that you'll be very good at that, Shar, affecting passion. And then DiMotta will cut those shots in with shots showing me and Cally engaged in various hot novelties. It will be kind of voyeuristic for you, Julian, but then you're a photographer."

"I'm not going to film any hard porn," Julian said.

"Why not?" Neil asked.

"Why?"

"Seriously, I'd really like to know why you refuse to film the sex sequences that DiMotta wants for his picture."

"And seriously, I'd like to know why I should. Tell me."

"Because you were hired to do a job."

"Not that job."

"Well, look Julian, just tell me what it matters if you photograph the sequences?"

"What does it matter if I don't?"

Neil grinned. "You keep answering my questions with questions."

"That's right. Why should I be pressed to explain to you why I refuse to film the porn? You're the advocate—you should tell me why I should."

"Neil, you jackass!" Sharon said. "Maybe Julian's telling you that he's thinking about his career. Maybe he's got principles, ever think of that? Why don't you just shut up."

"Principles?" Neil said. "I think that the two of you are confusing sex with morality. Sex can be a very liberating, very human sacrament."

"Oh, shit," Sharon said. "You're starting to sound like DiMotta's parrot."

"About time now," Julian said, stepping up out of the cockpit.

"Julian," Sharon said, "have you noticed that DiMotta has been cruising around and shooting film of you?"

"No."

"Well, he does. He circles around the barge and takes pictures of you taking pictures."

"Maybe," Neil said, "he's going to make a movie of people making a movie."

"That's original," Sharon said.

"Well, then maybe's he's going to shoot a movie of people shooting a movie of people shooting a movie."

"*That's* original."

"I want to see a little heat-drugged indifference this afternoon," Julian said.

Neil nodded. "You're seeing it now."

"Julian," Sharon said, "will you be going back with DiMotta again this afternoon?"

"I suppose so."

"Will you tell him that I'll do nude scenes as long as they're not vulgar? Nothing else. I told him myself, but I want him to hear it again. And tell him that there has to be a closed set—no one, but *no* one is to be out here who isn't working."

"I'll tell him."

"Go ye now, keeper of the flame," Neil said. "Do not soil thy lens with impure images."

"Keep your . . . chin up, Neil." Julian stepped over the lifelines, balanced for a moment, and then dove flatly into the water.

They quit early that day. Some towering black cumulus clouds were building in the northwest, and

DiMotta wanted the entire picture shot while the sky was clear. The sun was important to this movie, he said; the relentless sun. Climate was essential to mood; endlessly fine days were as depressing as endlessly dreary ones. He wanted to capture the feeling of monotony, the annihilation of time.

They were returning to the resort on the big cabin cruiser. Julian was sitting with DiMotta on the flying bridge. DiMotta enjoyed controlling the boat, and was good at it.

"I think you've succeeded in conveying monotony," Julian said.

DiMotta grinned. "Too much monotony?"

"Maybe so."

"The monotony is the prelude," he said. "It is the calm before the storm. There will be an eruption, an explosion of action soon—you'll see. The monotony is essential to my purpose; it will lull the audience, perhaps bore them, and what follows will electrify them. I'll tear their nerves out at the roots. Shock, the unexpected, the abrupt transition from monotony to horror—that's what I'm after."

"I suppose the sex will prevent them from becoming too bored," Julian said.

He nodded. Then: "Neil told me this afternoon that you refuse to film the erotic sequences."

"That's right."

"But they will not be pornographic."

"No?"

"No, they're a part of the prelude—no, not the prelude, the post-prelude. Tender and violent sex, animal and lyrical sex, the transcendent quality of sex, and the solace."

"Yes?" Julian said, smiling.

"The sex will first be filmed as an act of mindless

passion, a venture toward the abyss, an act related to murder. And then photographed in slow motion, very slow, intimate, gentle. And in editing I will cut back and forth between the two, first the frenzy, then the tender balletic fusion of two bodies, the frenzy again, and so on."

"You'll get an X-rating," Julian said.

"Is that what occurs to you?" DiMotta said scornfully. "Do you think that I care about Hollywood's rating system? Do you believe that I make films for the popcorn eaters, the beer drinkers at drive-ins?"

"Where is the Mexican cameraman you promised you'd hire?"

"There is not a good man available at the moment. You and I shall have to finish filming the story."

"Okay. But I'm not going to film the sex sequences."

"Why not?"

"Because to you it may be all the things you've said, tender and violent, animal and lyric, a balletic fusion of two bodies, but to every one else it's just going to be screwing."

"Sharon also has refused to cooperate," he said bitterly.

"That will teach you to hire philistines," Julian said.

"But you'll stay?"

"I'll stay."

"Good."

"But I don't want a screen credit."

"As you wish."

"It's not just the porn, Alfredo. I don't like the way you work. You go it alone. I can't plan a shot because I never know what it is until I report for work in the morning. I can't impose style on this picture, your style and my style, because your concept changes from day to day. I am excluded. You hired me to be your cinematographer, but you won't let me do my job."

"I've given you freedom."

"No. You're always talking about freedom, always, and then you ensure that there isn't any available."

"Nonsense!"

"It's true."

"Give me one example of how I might have interfered with your work."

"I've already given you examples. I'll give you one more. You are acting as a cameraman. Right? But you never consult me. You don't respect my knowledge or authority. You do as you please. Do you believe that I would permit our mythical Mexican cameraman to film on his own? Of course not. I was hired as director of photography. But you—has it ever occurred to you that you should submit to my authority whenever you pick up a camera?"

"Listen," he said, "listen you, this is *my* picture. I conceived it, I financed it, I cast it, and by Christ I will make it according to my whim."

"Exactly," Julian said. "I don't want a credit."

eleven

MEMORANDUM #8

DI-SAUK PRODUCTIONS   "THE DEATH FIRES"

TO: Mr. Frederick Saukel, Mr. Neil Warden, Miss Sharon Saunders, Mr. Julian Campbell.
FROM: Mr. Alfredo DiMotta.

Friends,

On Monday we commence our second week of filming. A certain mood has been established, and now we must smash that mood and create another, different, more powerful and perhaps more dangerous mood. Now we must begin to acquire the creative momentum necessary to carry this project on to—let me say it—a curious and wonderful conclusion, art.

I shall be demanding more from everyone. I shall demand, first of all, that you surrender your habitual quirky individuality, sullen rebellions, and obstructive concepts of personal freedom. We must now become a unit, a single entity, a "team" in American parlance. But really, it should be more than that. We must temporarily fuse ourselves into a kind of symbiotic organism, a great creature composed of many small creatures, with a single will and ego. Think of me as the head of this creature, and yourselves as my arms and legs and eyes and ears, my living tools. I cannot proceed without you. Nor can you go on without me. So I ask you to submit and thereby become whole.

I know that some of you have complained about our first week's work; some have already adopted their old reflexes of defeat and failure. I understand. It is painful to dare. I, more than any of you, realize how difficult it is to endure the agony associated with the death and rebirth of the personality. But I am asking that you venture into unknown and hazardous forms of expression. I am asking you to become new. Have courage. Stretch out, reach, exceed your limits for the purpose of establishing new limits. Die a little now in order to live later at a higher pitch.

Julian and Sharon—you have refused to cooperate in filming scenes that I believe absolutely essential to this picture. You are paralyzed by out-of-date myths; frozen by old concepts of morality.

This, my friends, is not 1916.

I ask that you two reconsider. I can and will film those brief, beautifully erotic sequences without you, but the movie will be poorer without your participation.

Sharon, Julian, dare this once—break the prejudices that bind you, seek liberty. I promise you this: The carnal episodes will be thunderous in innocence, reverberant in purity, transcendent in beauty. Sex as the only true human sacrament—can you appreciate that in your heart of hearts?

Sharon, you have a great opportunity to pioneer, a vital chance to serve; your body, your beauty can contribute to startlingly new perceptions of the sexual act, which is today in danger of becoming trivialized. I have no desire to manufacture just another pornographic movie. No! No, I swear that it is my goal to destroy base, vulgar pornography with a lucid, quasi-religious celebration of sensuality. I mean to sing of love.

And Julian, I require your cold lyricism for these "hot" scenes, your detached and icy attention to form, design, composition. Only you are capable of "cooling" these scenes as I wish. I believe that you are capable of imposing an almost symphonic order upon the chaos of abandoned sexual experimentation; and you, perhaps, can lend clarity to the wildly fragmented images and hallucinatory fever of madness.

Sharon, Julian, trust me. I am a vandal, yes, but I only destroy in order to create anew.

Dare with me to witness the unspeakable and monstrous—the new.

I am certain that we will make a fine motion picture. A revolutionary motion picture. I believe that the resistance that I see now is a sign that we are all desperately struggling against—or toward—difficult truths.

It is a cliché, but true, that one pays for everything. But I myself am confident that the cost of denying self-revelation is greater than the expense of accepting it. Surrender can be a supreme victory.

Remember: "There is no such thing as moral phenomena, but only a moral interpretation of phenomena." Nietzsche.

Alfredo

Julian and Sharon were bored by that night's movie (Antonioni's *Red Desert*) and in the middle went to the bar for a drink.

"What did you think of DiMotta's memo?" Sharon asked.

Julian shrugged. "Another polemic. DiMotta's persuasion approaches coercion."

"He talked to me for about an hour this afternoon, after I'd read the memo. The way he talked—it was like I was being invited to do something holy, like maybe give birth to the baby Jesus."

Julian smiled and nodded.

"You know, at first I believe that I can understand what the man is saying, but after I consider it for a while I realize that I don't understand at all."

"DiMotta uses the language in a very personal way."

"Right. It's mostly smoke."

"It's the abstractions," Julian said. "He's a mystic, and mystics have to be abstract. If they expressed themselves in a straightforward way, everyone, including themselves, could tell they were bullshitting."

"Okay, but the memo and what Alfredo said to me afterward seemed to make some sense. Really. I mean he pretty well had me convinced to do the scenes. I considered it, I damned near said yes."

"But you didn't."

She was quiet, and then: "A part of me wants to follow Alfredo."

"Follow him, then."

"If only he'd tell me where he's going."

"He doesn't know."

"Do you think that's true?"

"Yes."

"But he seems so sure, so absolutely certain. Sometimes he makes me feel like I'm a child and he's an adult—that he *knows* so many things that I don't know.''

''Watch out,'' Julian said.

''He seems to know and understand me so well, my deepest secret self.''

''Sure, that's the mystic—he pretends to know things we don't know, have powers that we don't have.''

''He really may be a deep man, Julian.''

''He isn't.''

''How do you know that he isn't?''

''How do you know that he is?''

''But I mean—he knows things that we don't know. He's gone farther out than we have, much farther, and he's come back different from other people. He can maybe guide us toward a new level of awareness.''

''Crap,'' Julian said.

''Oh, babe, I'm so confused.''

''DiMotta is just another salesman.''

''But what is he selling?''

''Himself, like all good salesmen. His product is Alfredo DiMotta.''

''No, there's something special in him, honestly there is. I don't know what the specialness is, but it's there. Maybe he really is a genius.''

''That's what he likes people to think.''

''He has a very powerful personality.''

''So do any number of quacks and psychopaths and pimps.''

''I fight him all the time. But it's hard, and I get a little weaker all the time.''

''Yes?''

''When he tried to persuade me to do the scenes I had an awful hard time remembering why I didn't want to do them. My arguments sound so silly and prudish in my ears, absurd. Really, why *won't* I do the sex stuff?

If the scenes are done the way Alfredo says they will . . . I'm not a virgin. Am I going to be *despoiled?* A part of my mind says, why not? What can it hurt? My mind even tells me that it may be exciting, doing things like that for the camera. Okay? My mind almost gave up and said yes to Alfredo. But my stomach turned.''

"Listen to your stomach. It's smarter."

She smiled. "You don't feel it? The force of his personality?"

"No," Julian said.

"Not at all?"

"None. He just irritates me. Like a salesman who insists that I buy a pair of shoes two sizes too small for me.''

"Oh, he'd love that comparison."

"I think I can see why women might be vulnerable to DiMotta's con. Most women are looking for some kind of self-transcendence, exaltation, and DiMotta promises those things. In twenty thousand words or more. Men are more practical.''

"Now it's my turn to say crap."

"Men are vulnerable to the promise of power, real power that they can wield. DiMotta has no power to share. Only a kind of pathetic pseudo-power."

"No, you're wrong. He has a real power. I don't know what it is exactly, but he has power."

"To hell with DiMotta," Julian said. "Do you want another drink?"

t w e l v e

Dear Julian:

I was pleased to receive your letter, of course, but disturbed to read—mostly between the lines—that you are still troubled by the obscure anxiety, dread, guilt, etc., that you spoke about during that long night in June.

And poor Michael Callaghan. How ghastly, how sordid. My God, it is beginning to appear that all of us will die violently in a fleabag hotel or on a dark street or lonely beach. Callaghan is number three. That is, he is the third of my acquaintances to be murdered in the last year. How can that be? What barbaric times these are!

I'll attempt to answer your queries as well as I can now, and then consult a few friends and see what else I can learn.

First, you asked my opinion of Alfredo DiMotta's

pictures. Yes, certainly I have seen his three feature-length films (he also made two short documentaries in Argentina years ago, but there are no prints available), but I can't flatly tell you that they are good or bad, because they are both. DiMotta is uneven: occasionally brilliant, with touches of actual genius here and there; often banal; and sometimes just fraudulent artistically and intellectually. It seems to me that the man assigns equal value to all of his ideas; he does not—or cannot—discriminate. A tea party and mob violence (La Noche Triste), erotic love and sadomasochism (Sal Si Puedes), the random, almost bland cruelty of children and the malevolent, calculated cruelty of the totalitarian state (A Díos, Rafael)—they are all presented in the same tone, given the same weight and emphasis, created (it seems to me) out of a terrifying moral vacuum. DiMotta has never invented a character, not even a child, who was not totally corrupt. (The concept of evil children is very fashionable these days, of course; our collective self-loathing is without limit.)

Still, every now and then DiMotta succeeds in matching his sterile vision of life to what is genuinely sterile and degrading in all of our lives; he bullies us into sharing his nausea. Perhaps those moments are accidents whose odds can be mathematically calculated, like the chance of three lemons coming up on a slot machine; but it does happen, and when it happens it works beautifully in a lunatic, comedic way.

DiMotta has made some two- or three-minute sequences that are as bitterly, outrageously funny as anything ever done in film. It doesn't happen often enough, though, because although DiMotta is rigidly faithful to his vision, his vision, I believe, is not always faithful to life.

Yes, you are right, his films are bad technically, but

*he was forced to make them on a shoestring. He will
certainly do better now that he has adequate financing.*

*DiMotta has a small cult following that may very well
increase. He might develop into a new Buñuel. I doubt
it, though; each of his pictures has been slightly less
ordered, less restrained, less intelligent than the previous. I think he is losing his touch, in that he can no
longer force us to share his very private obsessions.*

*No, until I read your letter I had not heard that he
has made pornographic films.*

*Yes, I am familiar with the work of Sharon Saunders.
She appeared in a number of cheap beach rip-offs, wrig-
gling and twisting around the driftwood fires in a small
bikini. And I have seen her in two or three television
movies. She is a beautiful girl, with a charming awkwardness, an appealingly ugly voice, and an élan vital
that made all the other actors around her look like plastic dummies. You suggest that she is not an actress. I
disagree. I think she might do very well in comedy,
where her awkwardness, her voice, her vagueness and
vulnerability might be extremely effective. She has been
poorly cast so far. She is absolutely not a dramatic actress. But in comedy . . . yes.*

*Julian, don't underestimate DiMotta; he is not a stu-
pid man, and he very well may have selected Miss Saunders for the role because he recognized her comedic
talent. DiMotta makes comedies, black screwball satires,
acid parodies. You should not be deceived by the surface
gloom, the slow pace, the apparent social concern, etc.
Alfredo DiMotta is indulging in a private mirth.*

*Neil Warden. He could be very good. But they're try-
ing to promote him as a Brando or Dean, and he will
never project their kind of power. There is a sullenness
in Warden's rage; a lazy man concealed behind the in-*

tensity; triviality seeps through his pain. Yet he is more than competent.

And you inquired about a man named Frederick Saukel. I only know what you told me that June night; that he was rich, corrupt, physically ill, that you had attended a few of his parties and found him wholly contemptible. I will make some inquiries.

Now, Julian, I hesitate to comment on things outside of my authority (a lie), but yes, brain damage can radically alter behavior. Of course. Brain trauma, tumors, reduced circulation, etc.—all can have considerable effect upon the personality. But you know that, your physicians have been candid.

Did you not tell me that the doctors had informed you that you had suffered minimal brain damage? And that within a few weeks your EEG's were of little concern to the doctors? Well?

I know even less about "amnesia" than I do about neurology, but that won't stop me. Were you in one of your fugue states during our conversation last June? Do you recall our talk?

I suspect that that is so. Well, I can assure you that your behavior was in no way alarming. You seemed agitated, intense, confessional, but you were still basically the same Julian that I have known for years. You were Julian in another mood, that's all.

Let me play Herr Doktor for a moment.

You have always had a strong tendency to suppress any display of emotion, be stoic, self-sufficient, undemonstrative—refreshing qualities in these days of narcissistic whining and gut-spilling and primal-screaming and group-encountering and letting it all hang out and being up-front, etc., all the fashionable inhibition-stripping whose goal is a return to infantilism. Okay.

But perhaps your stoicism has not proved adequate

in coping with the enormous stress resulting from the accident and its aftermath, i.e., your long physical and mental recovery. And most important, supreme, your guilt. And there is guilt. Four died, only you lived. A drunk could not control his vehicle and there was a head-on crash. There was nothing that you could do, nothing. You know that. I know that. Everyone knows that except your "Midnight Stranger."

So many terrible things happened to you in so short a period that you were not able to cope effectively in your natural way. Think of it, man: Your life was proceeding smoothly on a predetermined course, you were in superb health, you were becoming established in your chosen work, you were engaged to be married to a lovely woman, planning a family, nothing ahead of you, it seemed, but an ordered and rewarding life.

And then, my God, it was all suddenly and gratuitously gone. Your best friend and his wife are dead, your fiancée is dead, your health impaired for many months, even the functioning of your brain in jeopardy. Too terrible, too much. I do not know of many who could have handled this general horror better than you. But courage alone was not enough. It almost always is, but this time it was not. You fought as long as you could, silently and alone, as is your way, and then perhaps there was a slight schism in your psyche, a tiny fracture, an outlet through which the accumulated emotions could escape and thereby relieve the pressure. Do you understand?

I am suggesting that you suffered, and probably still are suffering, what you laymen call a "nervous breakdown." (And what we Herr Doktors might choose to call by a more sinister name.) Nothing to be ashamed of. It can happen to anyone. Etc. So then, is it possible, Julian, that your blackouts are the only means available to you to escape from your excessive self-domination and free a facet of your personality that is otherwise denied expression?

In your letter you wrote jocularly about the Midnight Stranger, but I know that you fear him. But you are the Midnight Stranger, my friend. He *is* you. Trust him— yourself. The more you fear him (yourself) *and* his (your) actions, the less likely it is that you will become reconciled. A house divided against itself...

Now I must make it clear that the above is merely informed speculation (informed where events prove me correct, speculation where my ignorance is demonstrated).

You really should consult your physicians. Maybe it would be best if you left the picture as soon as DiMotta can obtain a suitable replacement for you. Your health is more important than DiMotta's cinematic self-indulgence. It could be that you returned to work too soon.

Excuse the long and opinionated and not particularly lucid letter.

Best Wishes,
Lewis

thirteen

On Monday, Tuesday, and Wednesday, Julian shot some more footage of Sharon and Neil on the deck and in the interior of the sailboat, using the sound crew to record their idiotic dialogue. DiMotta encouraged them to improvise lines like: "The sea tastes us when we swim," and, "I am just beginning to remember what I've always known." Tuesday afternoon, giddy and rebellious, they began to invent a language that contained a preponderance of the syllables *ish, ack, ook* and *oosh*. And during the final thirty seconds of filming they sat on the deck and, straight-faced, recited all of the obscenities they knew.

On Thursday the area was closed to the villagers and those members of the cast and crew who were not essential to the filming. Sharon removed her bathing suit and Julian photographed her as she moved around the boat and pretended to perform a number of routine tasks. She was very shy at first, awkward, but after a time she began to move more naturally. She cooked on the Primus stoves, polished brass, braided strands of rope, sunbathed, combed her hair, swam.

And on Friday Sharon, wearing her bikini bottom, and Neil, in his swimming shorts, were filmed while embracing on a cabin berth and on the deck. Julian took close-ups of her face while she "affected great passion." She refused to simulate sexual intercourse. DiMotta, furious, said that he would edit these innocent scenes so skillfully into the erotic sequences that everyone would believe that Sharon had done it all. "You will see yourself on the screen doing things you never dreamed of," he said.

Sharon replied that it would take more than skill, it would need magic to convince an audience that that hippie pig's face and body were *her* face and body.

DiMotta himself photographed the pornographic sequences during the following week; Julian and Sharon were not on call.

Julian had often noticed a sixteen-foot skiff on the beach. It was old but beautifully designed, with a high sharp prow, considerable sheer, and a graceful stern. It had been rigged for sailing; there was a spruce mast, unstepped now, with the mainsail wrapped around it. The stainless steel shrouds and stays, neatly coiled, were attached to the spar. The rudder, now lying in the bottom of the boat, could easily be fastened over the stern with gudgeons and pins. The jib was tucked back under the bows along with a toolbox, steel bucket, anchor, and line. Julian inquired and found that the boat belonged to the hotel. Duane Poole said that Julian was welcome to borrow it. One of the fishing captains advised him on the tides, the best time to start for the island and when to leave it, and cautioned him to be alert for squalls— they sometime came up very swiftly at this time of year, and the waves could be dangerous in the shoal waters around the island.

Julian and Sharon went sailing every day that week (and on weekends after that). They found a small, secluded beach on the south end of the island and went there to picnic, swim, snorkel through the shallows, dig clams and steam them, and on Wednesday, and the days after that, make love on the beach.

DiMotta again flew to Los Angeles for the weekend; he said that he was doing some preliminary editing of the picture.

Saukel and the hominids stayed to themselves. Several times Julian had attempted to start conversations with the hominids, but they were mocking and contemptuous of him when together, and almost shyly inarticulate when alone. When one of them did speak it was in borrowed jargon; drug slang, a confused argot of pop psychology and misunderstood, trivialized Hindu and Buddhist mysticism.

On Saturday Julian received a note from Lewis Wiggens. The newspapers had carried a story that stated that $40,000 had been deposited to Callaghan's Los Angeles bank accounts on the day of his murder. The transaction had been handled by a Swiss bank whose officials refused to divulge the source of the funds.

Lewis also said that all of his inquiries about Saukel and DiMotta had netted one rumor. DiMotta's mother had worked as a servant in Saukel's household many years ago, and had returned to Argentina with much more money than servants were usually able to save, and with a belly swelling with Alfredo. Saukel was almost certainly—according to the rumor—the father of Alfredo DiMotta.

Julian told Sharon, and she laughed and said that it ought to be true even if it wasn't. "I'll believe it," she said.

The Sunday evening movie was broken up by a thunderstorm, rain and hailstones mixed, stuttering lightning that arced from cloud to ground, and the crowd scattered up the beach. Julian and Sharon ran through the orchard to his cottage; inside he turned on a small nightlamp, pulled the plug on the air conditioner, and opened all of the windows.

"Want a drink?" he asked.

"Okay."

Hailstones clattered loudly on the tile roof. Julian, standing close to the south window, heard a noise like bacon sizzling, felt a tingling sensation on his skin, and then there was a bluish flash and a detonation that seemed to shake the earth.

"Jesus," he said. "That was close."

"Nature does not compromise with puny man," Sharon said, imitating DiMotta's accent. "We are not interested in the lightning itself, nor even in the forces that fuse to produce the lightning, but only in the existential moment of terror that is aroused by it."

Julian smiled. She was a good mimic. "I disagree with you, Alfredo."

"You do not disagree with me, you disagree with the immutable mathematical laws that some call God."

They took their drinks to the sofa. It was still raining, although the sounds of the storm were becoming more remote as it drifted toward the west.

"Smell the air," she said.

He did: a rich, fruity fragrance, moist and sweet.

"I am so tired of breathing dry, burnt air."

"It will be dry and burnt again tomorrow."

"But this is tonight. I want to talk. Shall I see if I can get some pot from Neil?"

"No."

"We'll drink too much, then."

"I've got a better idea."

"That too," she said, "but later, all right?" She smiled and again imitated DiMotta: "We shall have carnal episodes thunderous in innocence, reverberant in purity, transcendent in beauty."

"I'd prefer something a little sweatier."

Sharon quickly finished her drink and asked for another. "Make it strong. And turn off the light when you come back. It's easier to talk in the dark."

When he was sitting next to her again, she said, "Julian, it's right for us to talk now, isn't it?"

"Sure."

"I mean, we're lovers, aren't we, really, and not 'just good friends,' as they say?"

"Yes."

"Or am I just a handy body while we're stuck down here?"

"A super body, the best at this latitude."

"You first," she said. "I haven't had enough to drink yet."

They talked, or rather Julian talked, responding only to her questions at first, and then relaxing, trusting her, he drew the outlines of his life: a banally happy childhood and carefree youth, his interests, his education and work, his fiancée and their plans—the beginning of a solid structure that would remain standing throughout his lifetime and maybe a little beyond. And then of course there was the accident, loss. His injuries. And now, he didn't know, but it sometimes seemed that he was not going to succeed in putting himself back together again. She said that certainly he would, he was doing it now wasn't he?

Julian got up and mixed two more drinks in the darkness. It had stopped raining, but water continued draining from the roof and the trees outside. He could hear faint music coming from the restaurant.

"And then there are the fugues," he said.

"But they've gone away, haven't they? When was the last?"

"The night Callaghan was murdered." He returned to the sofa.

"You didn't tell me that."

"I know."

"Do you want to tell me about it now?"

He told her about that night, the quarrel with Callaghan, Callaghan then not appearing for work, he—Julian—filming out on the desert, sleep . . . And then abruptly, hours later, awakening waist-deep in the sea. Saukel there, mocking him, talking about his singing and "ablutions." Had he been washing away blood? And then the next day Callaghan's body had been washed ashore.

"Two, three hours missing from my life."

"Oh, Julian, surely you don't think that you killed Callaghan."

"I'm afraid that I might have. The time is right—there's a hole in my life, and a dead man whom I'd quarreled with."

"That's nonsense. Listen to me, you fool, you didn't harm Callaghan."

"How do you know that?"

"I know *you*."

"I wonder how many times that has been said to murderers."

"Jackass! It's not worth discussing further."

Later Sharon said that, yeah, she'd had things pretty good too for most of her life, though not as sappy-smooth as Julian; but nothing ever bad until she'd gotten married. She had married a son of a bitch, no need to detail the particulars, since he was a common ordinary everyday kind of son of a bitch such as you'll meet anywhere, anytime. Alternately up and down, pathetic and violent, promises and broken promises, himself a cheat but jealous of her—you know the kind. Good-looking, sharp dresser, spent money he didn't have, drove fine cars during those periods in between the re-possessions, showed promise, really, plenty of promise. He would connect tomorrow. He beat her sometimes. And then he would weep and beg for forgiveness, un-derstanding. She'd always been the one to understand; she had tried to understand him for two and a half years. What a fool.

They had a kid. The baby didn't look right. A boy, malformed physically, defective mentally. Hopeless, a monster. The doctors said the boy would not live long, eight years, maybe ten. He was in a home now and would never leave. There had never been anything like that in her family, her people were all as wild and healthy as wolves.

Sharon, a little drunk now, had been talking in her usual wry, tough style, but she faltered while talking about her son, finally said, "He's a fucking vegetable," and then she began to weep.

Julian persuaded her to come outside and walk along the beach. They walked for a couple of miles, returned to the cottage, and made love, and then slept entwined in each other's arms.

---

fourteen

CALL SHEET #11
DI-SAUK PRODUCTIONS, INC.
"THE DEATH FIRES"

UNIT CALL 8:30 A.M.   At Island   Monday
                                                 Aug. 13

ARTIST	CHARACTER	DEPART	MAKEUP	READY ON SET
"A"				
Neil Warden	The young man	7:15	7:40	8:30
Sharon Saunders	The young woman	7:15	7:40	8:30
Frederick Saukel	Mr. Morte	7:15	8:00	9:30

ARTIST	CHARACTER	DEPART	MAKEUP	READY ON SET
"B"				
Timothy Buckner	Tim	7:45	8:15	9:30
Jazz Hines	Jazz	7:45	8:15	9:30
Carline Hamm	Cally	7:45	8:15	9:30
E. Torrez	Tribe member	7:45	8:30	9:30
B. Palafox	" "	7:45	8:30	9:30
J. Guzman	" "	7:45	8:30	9:30
Maria Ortiz	" "	7:45	8:30	9:30
Lena Salazar	" "	7:45	8:30	9:30
The children (5)	" "	7:45	9:00	9:30

PHOTOGRAPHY:
   All systems should be transported to the location.

SOUND:
   All systems, all personnel.

PRACTICAL ELECTRIC:
   Same as above.

CATERING:
   Coffee and doughnuts will be available throughout the A.M. schedule. Lunch at 12:00. Soft drinks and coffee served during the afternoon hours.

TRANSPORTATION:
   The director and all technical personnel, and their equipment, should be prepared to depart for the location at 6:30 A.M. exactly. Transportation logistics are such that one trivial delay may snowball into a serious pro-

duction setback. Be ready. The boat schedules are precisely calculated. Workers will be available beginning at 5:45 to move and load equipment.

7:15—"A" category cast members, makeup and wardrobe, script girl and assistant director. Be ready for transport.

7:45—"B" category cast and all other personnel will board their boats at this time.

NOTES:

Photography, we shall begin filming in the cave late this week or early next week. Please test lighting in advance. It may be necessary to smear the cave interior with soot or some other substance in order to reduce reflections.

Sound, work with photography in preparing cave. Test and arrange acoustical materials, etc.

All, Tonight's entertainment film will be Huston's *Moby Dick*. A splendid failure.

They spent all of Monday filming what DiMotta called the "landing and the greeting."

The landing consisted of shots of Neil and Sharon paddling the yellow life raft in toward the northern edge of the island, stepping ashore (dressed in filthy torn rags), and walking barefoot a few yards up the stony beach.

They were greeted by Saukel, the hominids, and the Mexican extras. A few fatuous lines of dialogue were exchanged. (Saukel: "We have been waiting for you, friends. What delayed you?" Neil: "The wind." Sharon: "The sun." Saukel, smirking: "Time, yes?")

The hominids and extras were dressed in rags too, but Saukel was immaculate in a baggy white linen suit, wingtip shoes with spats, and Panama hat. He petulantly tapped the ferule of his walking stick against a rock as he spoke. He was cunning, whimsical, childish—Saukel playing Saukel playing Saukel.

They photographed those simple shots over and over again, changing the angles, altering the composition. The light increased, shadows shrank and then expanded again. Julian warned DiMotta that he would not be able to intercut all the separate shots, integrate them; the time lapse, the change in light would be obvious in the minute- or ninety-second sequence. DiMotta replied with one of his murky abstractions.

"Julian, there is a reality that is not indebted to the sun. We are attempting to peel back some shadows in the human mind—we don't care about the shadows on rock and water. I have great patience, Julian. I still am not totally convinced that you are a fool." And he walked away.

During the noon break he apologized to Julian for the "fool" remark, and then tried to flatter him.

"Your photography has been absolutely stunning. Electrical oceans, fantastical skies. You elucidate my concepts even as you deny them. Lovely work."

Julian found it more and more difficult to talk with DiMotta. It was like talking with a man on the other side of a thick plate of glass; most of the words got through both ways, but the intent, the nuances were lost. DiMotta listened courteously but, like a partially deaf man, did not wholly understand. And he spoke English well and yet somehow remained vague. His language was clear, but his concepts were not; he spoke with an almost scientific precision about the mystical.

DiMotta was the prisoner of a very special viewpoint, Julian thought.

That afternoon the Arriflex camera was mounted in the bows of a skiff, and Julian filmed the beach over and over again as he was being rowed ashore. These shots were to represent Neil's and Sharon's view of the landing. It was a difficult series; the oarsman had to row very straight and smoothly, and it was necessary for Julian to continually readjust the focus and then open the lens aperture when the camera entered shadow. DiMotta wanted the figures on shore to be dim at first, underexposed, and then when the boat left sunlight they should suddenly become "shockingly real."

The greeting party stood quietly on the beach as Julian filmed them. Saukel was a few feet ahead of the others, grinning evilly.

At three o'clock DiMotta changed the setup. He brought the technicians and much of their equipment into the picture frame; half a dozen men, the burning lights, crates, the sound console, coils of wire, stacks of wooden rail, the studio camera mounted on its tripod.

The greeting party stood quietly on their marks, the same as before; and behind and around them men worked, or pretended to work. And off to one side DiMotta, with the Bell and Howell, filmed Julian and the oarsman coming ashore.

On Tuesday Julian photographed the "feast" scene, with the "northern tribe" (there were other small tribes on the island, DiMotta said) sitting around a driftwood fire and eating roast kid. "Eat greedily, all of you," DiMotta said. "Red meat is rare in this place." And so they ate greedily.

Their hands and faces were greasy; eyes were half-closed; bloody juice spurted from the undercooked meat as they tore it with their teeth. The sound men moved their mikes in close to record the noises. Julian filmed dozens of five-second shots: faces, hands, eyes, the kid slowly turning on a spit, the fire flaring and changing colors as grease spattered.

All of the cast except Saukel, Neil, and Sharon returned to the resort early in the afternoon. The fire was

built up again, the lighting and sound equipment rear-
ranged, and Saukel improvised a long, rambling speech.

"... and so you will see that this is a queer place,"
he said in his most sly and mellow tones. "Death, you'll
learn, is the only form of altruism we practice." He
lifted a bloody chunk of meat. "Protein. You are protein.
So are we all." He grinned his wicked V-grin. "I am
your liaison with death. I mediate between the natural
and the supernatural. I am an emissary of the faceless
one. You!" he said suddenly, pointing toward the camera, "you are a young woman, proud and with a clean,
musky smell, a bearer of protein . . ."

In all, Saukel talked for nearly twenty minutes, pausing when the camera setup was changed, then resuming.

Then Saukel, exhausted, left the set, and Julian filmed
Neil and Sharon "responding" to the speech. They tore
at the meat, chewed, licked their fingers, lifted their eyes
to stare at Saukel (a little to the right of the camera lens).

DiMotta was pleased with the day's work. "Very
powerful, very good," he said. "But Sharon, to a certain
extent you are still acting. Please, it isn't too late for you
to *become*."

Sharon shrugged, looked away from him, then turned
back. "Alfredo," she said quietly. "Someone has to tell
you this. It isn't working. This stuff—it's awful. You
haven't got a picture, Alfredo. I'm embarrassed for
you."

He smiled. "Don't worry about the picture," he said.

"It's so sincere," she said, "and so hideously bad."

Julian, Sharon, and DiMotta had a very early call on
Wednesday. It was cool and still dark when they went
out to the island. The Red Tide had intensified during
the last week; the sea had a rusty hue in daylight, and
at night flashed like neon, flared brightly and then faded,
burned elsewhere. Plankton was beginning to kill the

reef fish; each high tide left hundreds of them scattered along the beaches, bloated and stinking.

It was still dark when they landed on the island. DiMotta, carrying a big flashlight, led them up a steep, rocky trail to the summit plateau. The eastern sky was just beginning to pale with false dawn when they arrived. Four men were sitting with their backs against a big rock, smoking and talking quietly. Apparently they had brought up the camera equipment, lights, batteries, reflectors, and props. DiMotta told them to return to the beach.

"What is all this about?" Sharon asked.

"Closed set, Sharon. Just the three of us."

"Why?"

"We don't have much time," DiMotta said. "I want to begin shooting as soon as the sky turns color. You'll find your chalk marks over there, Sharon. Undress, please. Undress and take that bow and quiver of arrows and go to your mark."

"Jesus," Sharon said. "What's going on now?"

"I had a dream some time ago. I dreamed of an archer, a Diana. I want to film that dream. Have you ever used a bow?"

"Yes," she said sullenly, beginning to undress.

"Julian," DiMotta said. "What do you think? Is the camera all right where it is now? I thought it would be good this way, with those black lavalike rocks silhouetted in the foreground, and Sharon standing over there, and behind her the sea and the sky."

"Looks okay," Julian said.

"If you want to change the setup . . ."

"Too late now."

A thin rose-colored blur had appeared along the rim of the horizon.

DiMotta led Sharon—naked now, the quiver strung

over her shoulder—to the marks and explained how he wanted her to stand. "Very straight, yes. Arch your back. Lift your chin a little. Yes, good. You are proud, haughty."

Julian walked over to them, gave Sharon the end of his tape roll, then backed away and measured the distance between her and the camera. He inserted a film magazine into the camera, selected a lens and a filter.

"Are you ready?" DiMotta called.

"No."

"Please hurry."

Julian moved forward and switched on the lights. "Shit," he said.

"What's wrong?"

"Goddamn it, DiMotta, why can't you tell me what you intend to shoot so I can work out the lighting? Where's the gaffer? I've never seen such Mickey Mouse operations."

"Won't the lights do as they are?"

"Sure, if you don't mind having Sharon look like a plastic glow-in-the-dark dashboard ornament."

Sharon laughed. "You blew it again, Alfredo."

"Can't you rearrange the lights?"

"Sure, give me half an hour." Julian turned off the klieg lights.

"Well, then, can we shoot in the natural light?"

"By guess and by God. Maybe the reflectors will help. Come over here and give me a hand setting them up. If this shot doesn't turn out, you've got yourself to blame. Why do you always pull this crap on me? I've got to set up the shots myself. Get it through your head that *I* can't work spontaneously."

They quickly set up the reflectors, and then Julian returned to the camera and began taking a series of light and color-temperature readings with his meters. The rose horizon line had swelled into what looked like a huge bubble, and then it slowly burst and shot streamers of scarlet and crimson and peach across the now-blue sky. The clouds glowed incandescently.

"I changed strings on the bow," DiMotta was saying to Sharon. "It doesn't have a strong pull now. Hold the pose for as long as you can. It will be tiring, but don't move."

Julian continued to take light and color readings.

The upper curve of the sun, bloodred and sharply outlined, appeared above the horizon line. A wavy red trail appeared on the sea.

"Get the hell out of the frame, Alfredo," Julian said.

DiMotta backed away. Sharon got into position, notched an arrow, lifted the bow and pulled back the string. The bow was nearly as tall as she.

"Camera," DiMotta said. "That's beautiful, Sharon, perfect. Hold that pose, please, hold it for as long as you can."

Sharon's face was in profile, her body square-on to the camera. She stood very straight. Her blond hair, haloed by the light, moved in the breeze.

"Ah, beautiful," DiMotta said. "Just as I dreamed it."

She stood with her feet placed about eighteen inches apart; her left foot was flat on the rock and angled forward, her right heel was lifted so that she balanced on the ball. Her breasts were raised and spread. The sun, visibly moving in relation to the horizon, was rising just ahead of her forward leg.

"You are Diana!" DiMotta said.

A glittering red river split the ocean in halves.

"A little longer, Sharon, hold it, please."

The composition was perfect, Julian thought; the living curves of the human body juxtaposed against the harder geometry of bow and arrow; the taut strings forming two sides of an equilateral triangle and merging with the tips of the parabolically curved bow, and both strings and bow cleanly bisected by the straight arrow shaft.

Three quarters of the sun was above the horizon now.

"Hold it, Sharon," DiMotta said. "Just a little while longer. Julian?"

"I think that sunlight's going to hit the lens in a few more seconds," Julian said. "Sharon should fire the arrow when I say 'now.' "

"Do you hear, Sharon? Just a few seconds more. Release the arrow when Julian says so, but hold the pose afterward, don't relax immediately."

The sun, through atmospheric distortion, seemed reluctant to separate from the horizon; the bottom flattened and the rest was elongated into a blazing red oval. Then it broke free and compressed, becoming round again.

"Now!" Julian said.

Sharon released the arrow.

DiMotta: "Hold it now, don't move."

And then sunlight struck the lens. Julian switched off the camera. "My, my," he said, and he laughed.

"Julian?" DiMotta asked anxiously.

"I don't know. If I got the light just so, and if the lab doesn't screw up, it'll be a spectacular shot. We've got to have luck."

Sharon tossed the bow aside and removed the quiver of arrows. "God, my arms are numb. My knees have turned to jelly. Look at my hands shake. I couldn't have lasted another instant."

"You did wonderfully," DiMotta said. "Thank you. And thank you, Julian."

"Don't thank me until you see the rushes. We could be sure of that shot if you had let me set it up. I don't like these surprises."

"I don't think I breathed for three minutes. Just look at my hands shaking. Julian, honestly, what do you think?"

"We'll have to wait and see."

"Come on now," she said.

"It'll be gorgeous," Julian said.

"I saw it just like that in my dreams," DiMotta said triumphantly. "No pose reveals the grace and beauty of the human body better than that of the archer. It had to be done, I had to do it."

Sharon started getting dressed. "What now?" she asked.

"The others will be arriving soon," DiMotta said. "We'll be filming in the cave. The tribe will dance around a fire. Do you dance well, Sharon?"

"Super," she said, pulling on her Levi's.

They filmed in the cave that afternoon and again on Thursday morning. Thursday afternoon and all day Friday, a farcical "war" took place on the summit plateau between the northern tribe and the "cannibals of the south." It was absurd, a vulgar comic opera; only DiMotta took it seriously.

fifteen

DiMotta returned from Los Angeles late Sunday afternoon and passed the word that he had a rough cut of the film and would be showing it at the restaurant at nine that evening. He did not want to show it on the beach, he said, because there were things in it that would shock and offend the puritanical villagers.

All of the cast and crew, curious and a little puzzled, were there for the showing. Two projectors had been set up partway down a hallway, and a screen, not fully opened, had been placed against the north wall. Julian and Sharon got drinks from the bar and sat at a small table in the front.

"A surprise for us, Alfredo?" Sharon asked.

"I think you could say that, yes."

DiMotta stood up a few minutes after nine o'clock

and walked over to the screen. He raised his palms and then slowly lowered them as the hum of voices diminished. He wore khaki hiking shorts covered with pockets and flaps and zippers, a safari shirt, and a choker of Indian beads. His feet were bare.

"All right," he said. "You are going to see a rough cut of the picture tonight. I have been working very hard during my weekends in Los Angeles to put this together. But remember, it is a very, very rough cut. There are no credits yet, no fades or dissolves, no montage, and of course, no music. It is very raw. Quick cuts only. This is not the picture that will someday appear in the theaters. It will take me eight months, perhaps a year, to edit the final version. You understand. You have all seen rough cuts before. Some of the shots you'll see tonight will probably not appear in the theater version. And there are shots not present in this cut that may very well appear later. It will be a long, arduous task, the editing. Still, what you will soon see is basically what we have been working toward."

He slowly glanced over the audience, pausing at this face, that one, then folded his arms and said, "The movie is completed. I have all of the footage I need. Now before you all begin quoting me the terms of your contracts, let me say that you will be paid in full. And there are bonuses. Frederick has been extremely generous. So, although we have completed our work much sooner than originally expected, none of you will suffer financially.

"I have chartered another small airplane and the exfiltration"—he smiled at the word—"will commence tomorrow. Schedules for the flights are available at the desk. Please inquire about your flight.

"Any questions? No? All right, then. The waiters will quietly serve drinks and sandwiches during the showing.

If any of you is bored with the picture, try to conceal it. Julian? Sharon?'' He smiled again. ''Bonus checks can be torn up.''

DiMotta went to a chair that stood against the wall a few yards to the right of the screen; he apparently intended to watch the faces of the audience rather than the film.

''All right,'' he called to the projectionist.

The conical beam of light leaped across the room and illuminated the screen. The room lights were switched off.

''Credits will appear in this opening shot,'' he said. ''In very small letters at the lower right-hand part of the screen.''

The rough cut opened with the shot of Sharon—naked, the bow fully drawn—standing on top of the island's summit plateau with the sun slowly rising behind her. She could not be seen clearly at first, was little more than a shadow, but then as the light dramatically increased, she emerged out of the background with an almost three-dimensional reality. She remained motionless. One might have supposed that it was a still picture except that her hair blew lightly in the wind and the sun slowly rose behind her and the clouds, incandescent reds and oranges, changed shape. The sea below was cobalt.

Someone—the gaffer, Julian thought—began clapping, and then another of the Mexicans joined in, and then nearly everyone in the room was applauding. Julian knew that the applause was for him and that he should acknowledge it in some way, with a raised hand or a joke, perhaps, but he would not. DiMotta had conceived and set up the shot; Julian, quickly improvising, had photographed it. The quality was only partly due to his skill and knowledge; the rest was a lucky accident.

The colors flared and deepened. The sun, seething and enormous, moved steadily in relation to the fixed horizon. An aureole of light was ignited in Sharon's hair. Her tanned skin gleamed with the colors of the sun and sky.

The sun flattened along its base, seemed for an instant to turn into a viscid, liquid oval, then it stretched and broke free. Sharon released the arrow. She lifted her chin as she watched its flight. A few more seconds and the picture exploded into radiating sparks of light, a flashing diamond brilliancy that hurt the eyes, and then darkness.

There was more applause. Sharon took Julian's hand and squeezed it. When light returned to the screen, Julian could see that DiMotta, in the corner, was grinning at him.

The next sequence was from the last scene in DiMotta's previous picture *A Díos, Rafael,* when the boy Rafael was teaching his little brother how to play soccer and at the same time trying to explain death. (Their father had been killed by the police during a riot.) The child, about five years old, regarded sport and death with equal solemnity, and sometimes confused the two. At moments it was like an old Abbott and Costello routine—*Who's On First?*—though underplayed and toughly sentimental.

"What's going on?" Sharon whispered.

A couple of the Mexicans began to whistle derisively. *Finis* appeared and a list of credits began to unroll. Then the screen within a screen went dark, and the camera slowly moved back to reveal a small theater. Its houselights were turned on. The camera changed angles. About twenty well-dressed persons in the theater audience began to stir; the women gathered their wraps and purses; the men slowly rose from their seats, blinking and smoothing wrinkles.

Cut to a close-up of Alfredo DiMotta. He is nodding, smiling faintly.

Cut to a fat, bald man who lisps and sprays silver flecks of saliva.

FAT MAN: "... just marvelous, Alfredo, it is ... epochal! Yes, yes (liking the sound of that word), you've captured the essence of an epoch—it's ... epochal."

DIMOTTA: (Bored, irritated) "Thank you."

FAT MAN: "And what are you going to do next?"

(A flash, almost subliminally perceived in its brevity, of Sharon the archer.)

DIMOTTA: "I don't know. I have an image, an idea, nothing more."

Later there were shots of a pensive DiMotta walking down a deserted beach; strolling down a busy market street (the same street the girl walked in *Sal Si Puedes*); pacing, nervous and tousle-haired, in his study. Cut into these shots were a number of briefly flashed images: Sharon the archer, again: a long shot of a derelict sailboat, the *Idler*; Neil, his back against the mast, taking a sextant sight; Sharon in the yellow life raft; two bodies locked in sexual union; a view looking down at Callaghan's corpse, sandy and dotted with flies. The last two inserts were so short that they appeared to be abstractions; recognition was delayed, dependent upon the retinal after-images.

DiMotta, standing on the end of the resort's pier, smoking a cigar and looking out toward the island.

And then came the first shots of the empty sea, the stars, the sailboat seen in a series of long and medium shots, and some close-ups of Neil—his "heat-drugged indifference."

Sharon alone in the yellow life raft. Sharon aboard the *Idler*: sleeping in the cabin berth, eating, drinking water, walking on deck. And then three take-outs as she talked to Neil about her conviction that all of this was a dream, actually a dream within a dream *ad infinitum.* "Each morning I awaken from the dream and find myself deeper within the same dream. The dream becomes more real every time I wake up, and my life more vague."

She blew the lines the first two times. Twice the slate board appeared on the screen with the name of the picture, the scene and take numbers chalked on it, and then the arm snapped down and the take was repeated. This time she laughed on the third "dream," turned her head and said, "Do I *have* to say this crap, Alfredo?" The slate board appeared again, and this time Sharon read her lines satisfactorily.

A shot of Julian operating his camera aboard the cluttered, sun-flashing aluminum barge; beyond him were Neil and Sharon on the sailboat.

Neil and Sharon clowning; babbling nonsensically in their invented "language," and then blandly reciting obscenities.

The first of the candid shots; Julian and Sharon playing tennis. The cameraman—DiMotta—had been concealed in the shrubbery around the number 13 cabaña. There had been someone with him using a directional microphone; you could hear the popping of the hit balls, and Sharon's giggles and apologies.

Then there were thirty seconds of Sharon nude on the sailboat, but it was footage that had been taken while she was still awkward and self-conscious; the later film, taken when she had overcome her shyness, had not been used.

A candid view of Julian and Sharon walking along the beach at sunset, the space between them and the camera blurred by the telephoto lens.

Saukel and DiMotta sitting in lawn chairs in the mottled light of the orchard. Birds chirp in the trees and you can hear the hushed breathing of the sea. The sound had not yet been synchronized with the images; lips moved, and the words followed an instant later.

SAUKEL: (eyes closed) "So you want to quit."

DIMOTTA: "I didn't say that."

SAUKEL: "You said it isn't working."

DIMOTTA: "I am disappointed. . . . I am not going to be able to realize my original conception."

SAUKEL: "Perhaps, Alfredo, perhaps the flaw is in your concept."

DIMOTTA: "No. I simply wanted to make a picture that would resemble—no, recreate—the *ambience* of a nightmare. I intended to appeal to the Jungian unconscious, slowly guide the viewer into a strange and powerful dream. Force him to suspend his critical faculties, his sense of logic, his normal sense perceptions—make him, for ninety minutes, experience the dream, and through the dream a kind of liberating anarchy. Now, dreams are very often absurd and confusing in their action, they are not bound by natural law or everyday logic. I clearly understood that this motion picture must remain faithful to dreams in this respect, that I could not avoid the confusion and absurdity, but . . ."

SAUKEL: (Opening his eyes and smiling slyly) "What you mean is that you are making an absurd and confusing motion picture instead of an absurd and confusing dream."

DIMOTTA: "I made a mistake in casting Sharon for the part of the girl. She is too practical, controlled, bourgeois. I wanted a touch of madness, a fey witch, and day after day she presents me with a suburban housewife. And Julian is wrong—too cold, too literal."

SAUKEL: "Fire them."

DIMOTTA: "No, I have decided to make the other movie. Two movies, really."

SAUKEL: "The documentary."

DIMOTTA: *"Cinéma vérité."*

SAUKEL: (Sneering) "A fart by any other name . . ."

Then there was a view of Julian and Sharon sailing the little skiff. Behind them the island, pulled close by the telephone lens, rose up and blotted out the sky. DiMotta's voice on the sound track: "Perhaps, if I concentrate on our two healthy, outdoor, middle-class Americans, our Prom King and Queen, I'll uncover a story of some interest."

The landing and greeting scene, taken over and over again: Neil and Sharon coming ashore in the dinghy, as photographed from the island beach; Saukel and the greeting party, as seen from the rowed skiff; a shot that contained the technicians and all of their equipment; shots in which DiMotta appeared, photographing the photographer.

The long, beautiful shot of Sharon atop the island with the sun rising behind her. The arrow is released. An explosion of silver light.

A quick shot of Callaghan's corpse on the beach.

The tribe eating the roast kid. Gluttony, greasy fingers and faces, spurting juices.

Julian and Sharon sailing toward the southwestern edge of the island.

The island war; a goofy parody, it seemed, of the old cavalry-versus-Indians movies. Quick cuts of arrows flying, warriors dying, men clutching their stomachs as they fall off rocks. Then a slow tracking shot through the corpse-littered battlefield. Julian's and Sharon's voices were on the sound track during this farcical war, their words edited from a conversation they'd had many days ago (it was obvious that their cabañas had been bugged). Julian hesitantly telling Sharon about the automobile accident, the death of his fiancée and good friends, his subsequent loss of confidence, of purpose; and Sharon quietly confessing that she'd had a child from her marriage, a hopelessly retarded boy who now and forever would be confined in an institution. As edited into the film, they each took turns speaking; there was no continuity in the dialogue, no give and take, no fumbling for words—it was just two voices interrupting each other to catalog their miseries self-pityingly. "My son's a fucking vegetable," Sharon said, and the camera paused on a dead "warrior," a young boy who could not resist grinning and slanting his eyes up toward the camera. And then Sharon began weeping. Her sobs were amplified, false-sounding, as the camera resumed tracking through the battlefield.

A long, slow panoramic shot of the beach; thousands of dead fish scattered over the sand, all of them bleached and bloated and bug-eyed. Sharon's weeping remained on the sound track.

The sex between Neil and the girl Cally on the sailboat was photographed in a very soft focus, blurred at moments, and hardly pornographic—it had been done comedically, with many take-outs and repetitions, broken into a dozen fragments by views of the slate board.

A shot of two dogs copulating on the beach. Unidentifiable noises on the sound track, a silence, and then Sharon's voice saying, "That was good."

The Mexican technicians, playing cards, drinking and laughing, at a table in the restaurant patio.

A telephoto shot of Julian and Sharon, naked, their backs to the camera, emerging from the water. They walk a few steps up the beach, turn toward each other and embrace, kiss, and then slowly settle onto the sand.

"No" Sharon suddenly cried. It was almost a scream.

"No, you can't do this." She rose from her chair. Her knees buckled and she almost fell back, but then she steadied herself. Her shadow appeared on the left side of the screen.

"Alfredo, you can't do this," she said. "No, you can't. . . . I'll get a court injunction . . . I'll sue. You—what kind of man are you? You can't—this isn't done. It can't be done to people."

Someone had turned on the restaurant lights.

DiMotta, relaxed, smoking a cigarette, one leg crossed over the other, smiled at her.

On the screen now, faint in the room light, was an image of Julian and Sharon making love on the beach.

Sharon tried to speak, failed, tried again and failed, and then turned and unsteadily moved among the tables toward the door.

DiMotta did not have time to rise more than halfway out of his chair. His legs were still bent and his torso leaning slightly forward when Julian hit him. There was a dull, wet kind of sound, and Julian felt the shock travel all the way up his wrist and forearm to the elbow. DiMotta's head struck the wall, and he was slumping when Julian hit him again, taking more time now, aiming at the juncture of jaw and neck.

Julian turned and saw that four or five of the Mexicans had Buckner, the big hominid, down on the floor and were beating and kicking him. Julian circled around them and went outside.

Sharon was walking slowly toward her cabaña. "Leave me alone now," she said.

"We might as well talk it out."

"Go away," she said quietly. "I want to be alone. Do you hear? I only want to be left alone."

"Sharon . . ."

"I hate you," she said coldly. "Oh, God, how I hate all of you."

She turned and looked over the sea. "Do you think it's safe? What about sharks?"

"We haven't seen any sharks, have we? We'll stay close to the boat."

She shook her head. "No, I really don't want to swim."

He watched her drink the beer. The skiff, revolving as it drifted, had left them exposed to the sun for intervals. His arms and thighs and face had turned a salmon pink, but Sharon, better protected by her tan, had only burned on her nose and cheekbones. Her hair, dried and tangled, was the color of straw. The whites of her eyes were bloodshot, but the blue pupils were clear.

"Come on," he said. "You'll enjoy a swim. We should have been taking dips all day. It'll cool us."

"Okay, I'll go swimming if you'll finish the beer."

"Deal," he said. There was about a quarter of the can left. He drank it and started to remove his shirt. "We won't dive in, the splash might attract something. The best way to get back aboard, I think, is to step up on the curve of the rudder. Okay, babe?"

She smiled. "You don't have to talk to me like I'm a sulky little girl. I feel much better now, really."

The water was cool and silky smooth on his body and tasted sharply of salt. He swam a dozen strokes away from the skiff and then turned, treading water.

"Come on."

Sharon hesitated, then undressed and slipped over the side. She swam to him.

"Marvelous, isn't it?"

"Jesus. I feel like the girl in DiMotta's movie."

"Forget that."

"The water's so deep it makes me dizzy. How deep do you think it is?"

"Maybe a half-mile. Or more, I don't know."

"We should stay closer to the boat," she said. "What if there are sharks down there?" She lowered her face into the water. Her hair floated out in a dark gold sunburst. Then she looked up, blinking. "You can't see much without a mask."

The skiff was slowly drifting away from them.

"I don't like this," Sharon said, and she swam back to the boat and climbed aboard.

Julian had a sensation of being delicately suspended over an abyss, and that any caprice of nature or a false move on his part would send him slowly spiraling into the purple depths. The skiff was about thirty yards away now.

"Julian," Sharon called. "Please come back to the boat."

He saw that there was no more than twenty inches of freeboard at the lowest point of the skiff's sheer; twenty inches repelling the infinite tons of water.

"Julian, please. I don't like to be alone here. Please."

The sky, the sea, the little boat, the two of them.

"You're too far away. What if there should be a shark?"

And then, with a feeling not unlike regret, he swam back to the boat.

The long, hot, bright blue day ended with a suddenness that startled them. It seemed that one moment they were drowsing in the stifling mid-afternoon heat and the next moment he looked up and caught the sun slipping rapidly into the sea. A green gold radiance flared along the western horizon and died with a flutter. And then they were immersed in a soft blue twilight that swiftly and imperceptibly became full night. The stars and planets were ignited. The skiff at waterline was surrounded by a ghostly green aura.

Sharon's mood had improved with the beer and the

swimming, but as soon as it became dark she began to withdraw again. She was not interested in talking: "The only thing I can think about is being here. And there's nothing to say about that."

An hour later she said she was tired and wanted to sleep. He spread the cushions over the ballast rocks, removed the mainsail, and made their bed. Sharon covered herself with the sail even though it was still very hot.

Julian lit a cigarette, puffed twice, and threw it away; the smoke irritated the dry swollen membranes of his mouth and throat.

By eleven o'clock the heat had abated enough so that he could sleep.

n i n e t e e n

The sun had already risen when Julian awakened the next morning. The air was cool. He was aware of a hushed ticking. He smelled gasoline and something else, a sweetish chemical odor—varnish? He sat up. The cabin cruiser floated nearby. DiMotta, beneath the flying bridge's canopy, was filming them; Saukel, wearing a bulky terrycloth robe and a triangular hat assembled out of newspaper, sat on one of the fishing chairs.

Saukel removed the cigar from between his teeth and beamed at Julian with sham astonishment and delight.

"Flotsam!" he crooned. "Well found!"

Sharon awakened abruptly, sat up and stared wildly at the boat.

"Jetsam!" Saukel cried. *"Ma chère amie!"*

Sharon stared at him. Her facial skin seemed to have

drawn taut overnight, and her eyes now appeared enormous. "You bastards," she said.

Saukel altered his expression, looked somber. *"Enfants perdus,"* he said with oily compassion.

And then Sharon began speaking rapidly, at moments incoherently, about her ordeal, her fear and suffering, first berating them and then gushing gratefully because they had at last returned.

Julian studied the cabin cruiser. It was a big boat with considerable freeboard; only the transom, cut low to facilitate hauling large fish aboard, was low enough to provide access from the water. DiMotta was filming Sharon with the Arriflex. There was probably a microphone somewhere on deck.

". . . it was cruel of you, terrible . . . an awful time . . . but thank God you've . . ."

Saukel was sitting just a few feet away from the stern, but he was old and sick, too weak to stop Julian without a weapon of some kind. There might be a weapon nearby, a gaff or a club for stunning fish, or a gun. Julian would have to take the chance.

". . . no food and almost nothing to drink . . ."

DiMotta would be slowed by the camera. It was not mounted, and no man who regularly used expensive photography equipment could just throw a camera aside; the reflex, even in a crisis, would be to find a safe place for it. Then DiMotta would have to descend the steep ladder to the deck, turn and rush toward the stern.

". . . so please, please, please stop your terrible game and . . ."

In one motion Julian sprung erect and dived over the side. He swam face down, kicking and pulling hard. Diving off the skiff had given him some distance, momentum a little more, and within a few strokes he could blurrily see the underwater section of the hull, red-painted and covered with gray green moss. He came in toward the stern at an angle. Now he could see the twin screws and the rudder assembly. Almost there, two more strokes. And then there was a sudden explosion of noise and bubbles, a huge silver cloud of them, and he was engulfed. Beyond the bubbles he could see the flashing propellers, feel their turbulence. The force increased, and for an instant he feared that he was going to be sucked into the screws, but then the boat drew away.

He surfaced, out of breath and with deadened limbs. Fool. There were controls on the flying bridge as well as below in the cabin. Still, if the engines had not caught immediately he would have made it aboard. He watched the cabin cruiser glide away. The engines were killed. DiMotta had the camera again.

He treaded water until he had regained his breath, and then swam back to the skiff and pulled himself up.

"Now do you see?" he said furiously to Sharon. "For Christ's sake, do you finally comprehend that they are not here to help us?"

She stared at him.

"That, in fact, one way or the other they're going to see us dead?"

She was pale beneath her tan; her complexion was yellowish. A change in her inner state had effected an obscure change of expression; her separate features had somehow lost their special harmony, each seeming isolated, and now her chin appeared too sharp, her nose too small, her eyes too wide apart, her lips too thin. She looked like an adolescent girl who might grow into either beauty or ugliness.

"I'm sorry," he said.

She averted her eyes.

"We're not out of it unless you quit. DiMotta probably expects us to turn into cannibals or something.

Don't give in to despair. Whatever you do, don't beg anymore. Okay?''

She nodded.

"Okay, Sharon?"

"Yeah, okay."

There were clouds this morning, thin cirrus formed in long parallel bands, but not enough breeze to more than ruffle the water's surface from time to time.

All night they had drifted, toward the mainland if the direction of the current remained constant. He estimated that they were drifting at around one and one-half or two knots. They might be more than halfway across the gulf now. The current might change directions at any time, of course, curve southward toward the mouth of the Pacific. And the regular change of tides might affect their speed and course. Still, there was a good chance they would be in sight of land by tomorrow.

There were patches of pale green weed floating on the surface; occasional pulsing jellyfish; and once Julian lifted his eyes in time to see three flying fish rupture the water's smoothness, spread their membranous fins and soar for fifty feet before splashing home. He thought about fishing but then decided that neither he nor Sharon were thirsty and hungry enough to keep down raw fish.

The sun was climbing, growing hot. Its brightness and heat did not seem much affected by the wispy veils of cirrus. He rigged the awning and coaxed Sharon back into the shade. She moved listlessly and with what appeared to be excessive regard for her balance.

"Want to swim?" he asked her.

"No. Later, maybe."

"When?"

"Later."

The cabin cruiser was some distance away now; it seemed to be drifting at a slightly slower rate than the skiff. DiMotta was still up on the flying bridge; Saukel was in the cabin now, cooking bacon. The air above the stove's T-shaped exit tube was blurry with the rising heat, and Julian could smell the spicy odor of bacon. The monotonous odors of the sea seemed to have purified his sense of smell; wood, gasoline, and varnish, and now the bacon were so strongly fragrant that he felt that he had never truly perceived those odors before.

His sense of smell was extraordinarily acute then, but his eyes were failing him; they were sore from the sun-glare and salt water, and there was a kind of smoky white haze on the periphery of his vision. He supposed that his eyes were as bloodshot as Sharon's; networks of red veins in a filmy red wash.

He had been sweating for some time and now he noticed that Sharon too was beginning to perspire.

"Okay?" he said.

She looked at him, nodded, closed her eyes again.

At midday Julian felt the beginning of a headache, a tiny burning seed that seemed to originate three inches behind his eyes. He visualized it as a minute glowing dot in the center of his brain. Sometimes it went away without getting worse, but usually it expanded and divided, spread tentacles to his eyes, temples, jaw—like thirty-two toothaches—and the base of his skull. And with the headache came weakness, nausea, and a kind of delirium.

The heat intensified; his eyes wept from sun-glare and pain; the air seemed to thicken.

Two or three times the engines were started on the cruiser and DiMotta moved to a new position. Julian did not pay much attention; he didn't know when DiMotta filmed them or even if he filmed them at all. It hardly mattered.

His mouth had been dry all night and this morning,

but now it contained a bitter white secretion. He spit many times over the side, and finally his mouth was dry again, but even more bitter-tasting, and his tongue was numb.

Vaguely, as from a distance, he heard Sharon moaning. He did not want to come out of himself, reenter the world; it was all he could do to endure his headache and sickness without attending to Sharon's misery as well. But finally, reluctantly, he opened his eyes.

She was bent double, her eyes closed, teeth bared, squeezing her right calf with both hands.

"What's wrong?"

"Cramps."

She had stopped perspiring; her complexion was still yellowish, and her skin had a dry grainy look, like paper.

Julian went forward into the bow. He took an empty beer can and filled it halfway with water; then half filled another can with sea water. He emptied the salt water into the fresh and returned to Sharon.

"The cramp's gone now," she said.

"I'm afraid I haven't been taking very good care of you."

"I've had other cramps. That was the worst."

"This won't taste especially good. It's half fresh and half sea water."

"But I thought it was bad to drink sea water."

"This much will do you good. You've sweat the salt out of your system. That's why you're getting cramps. Drink this."

"I can't hold it, my hands are shaking too much."

"Christ, I've let you dehydrate. I'm sorry. Here, I'll hold the can. Take it in small sips." He helped her drink.

"It doesn't taste bad," she said. "Not too salty."

"It probably tastes okay because you need the salt so much. You'd get sick from it at any other time."

"Where are they now?"

"To the west. About fifty yards away."

"Is DiMotta filming us?"

Julian shaded his eyes. "Yes," he said. "He's shooting with a telephoto lens. Close-ups, no doubt—do you want to put on some makeup? And Saukel is aiming the shotgun mike this way, but I don't think that unit will pick up our voices clearly at that distance. But we should talk quietly."

"They've got to be crazy, just crazy."

"Do you want some more water?"

"I feel much better now. You have some."

"Later."

"You look awful," she said. "Do I look that bad? I suppose I do. The nightmare life-in-death, at last. I can't believe that I'm going to die, Julian, I simply can't accept it. But it's true, isn't it?"

"No, it isn't true. Look at those clouds. We're going to get wind, maybe a storm. At night, in a storm, we might be able to get away."

"Sure," she said. "I bet we do." She didn't believe it.

t w e n t y

Three o'clock. The parallel rows of cloud continued to fly from southwest to northeast, and the sun dimmed and brightened with a kind of strobe effect. Long, undulating bands of shadow skimmed swiftly over the water. And there were occasional breaths of wind now, brief furnace exhalations that arose and died within a few seconds. The water smoothed after each flurry.

Julian drowsed beneath the awning. His head throbbed, a hammer blow with each heartbeat. He was half-blinded by the pain.

Eyes closed, he let his mind drift aimlessly, aware only of sensations; and then he began to see familiar images, hallucinatory in clarity, dream-like in their powerful evocation of mood. He saw the long hallway, the spatter of shadows on the wall, the obscene carvings on the double doors. And then he hallucinated aurally, he could hear music and voices rising from below. The sounds and images sharpened. The doors slowly swung open, and room light spilled out onto the hall floor in a growing wedge. Naked humans in animal masks: two foxes and a cat, women; a wolf, a hyena, and two birds of prey, men. Then two of the women's masks were gone, one of the foxes and the cat, and there were screams, the flashing falling knives, blood and screams. The woman with the carmine lipstick and fingernails, and the small blonde with a cast in one eye were being murdered.

Julian opened his eyes. It all came flooding back to him. He remembered, and was innocent.

The empty spaces in his life, the fugue periods, were almost filled; there were still small gaps, details, events of no importance, the kind of things that are lost to normal memory. But the essence . . .

He remembered himself as he was then, desperately cheerful, more open to people than he had ever been, a little wild in his pursuit of emotional release. He could vaguely recall the girls he picked up in bars; a couple of fights, with one encounter with the police; Saukel's garish weekend parties; Saukel himself, and DiMotta, Sharon, Callaghan, Neil, even the hominids, and many others. The music, dancing, noise, the vulgarity and absurdity, the undercurrents of violence and anarchistic sex.

The murder film. He had not witnessed or photographed the murders, as he'd feared, but he had seen the film. His nightmares were a distorted version of the movie scrambled with some actual events and impressions.

One of the parties. Hard rock music, men and women dancing convulsively in the flashing strobe lights while others—some in evening dress, others in rags—stood in the corners or wandered the perimeter of the huge room. Eyes like stones. Mouths like fresh wounds. You kept walking into walls of hatred. Callaghan, half drunk, one eye closed against the rising smoke from his cigarette, was shouting to be heard above the noise. He had found something in Saukel's film library, a Japanese picture that no one had ever heard of, it wasn't even dubbed, couldn't understand a word, but Jesus, pal, the photography was great, as fresh as rain and smooth as an egg. You want to see it, come over at eleven in the morning Wednesday, Saukel and DiMotta will be gone all day, they'd have the place to themselves. Okay? Don't forget, eleven on Wednesday.

That was another blank night; Julian forgot everything, the party, Callaghan's offer, Sharon—that was the night he had gone home with her. Callaghan, sarcastic and already half drunk, telephoned him at noon on Wednesday. Julian, after questioning Callaghan and learning about the Japanese film, apologized for forgetting, mentioned his fugues, and said that he would be there soon. He had to ask for directions.

One of the servants guided Julian up to the third floor studio. Callaghan had covered the windows and set up the projector and screen. They sipped Saukel's best cognac and watched the Japanese film. Julian did not believe that the photography was much better than average.

Then Callaghan went into the film vault and returned with a reel containing the famous palace steps sequence of *Potemkin*. They watched that, and then one of the pornographic films that had been made in the studio. It was plotless, pointless, just a well-photographed orgy. Julian recognized some of the participants, others were masked. "If I told you who some of those people are, pal, you wouldn't believe me."

Julian was drunk then too, and bored, and thinking about going home when Callaghan emerged from the vault with the kind of sturdy boxes that are used for the transportation of reels of film.

"What the hell's this?" Callaghan said. There were no markings or address labels on the box. He had found it in the safe with the really valuable old movies. The safe had not been locked as usual. Then he remembered; this was the package that had come up from Argentina in the diplomatic pouch. DiMotta had a friend at the consulate, and the guy had personally delivered this. Callaghan had been present at the time and had assumed that it was a print of one of DiMotta's own pictures. But the name of the laboratory was not stamped on the box, there were no markings at all. And why should film come into the States in the diplomatic pouch? And why had it been kept in the safe?

Negative, the master print, and another print. It was short.

Night. The camera slowly tracked down the long hallway, paused to examine the door carvings, and then the doors swung open. The bright lights. Seven persons, in masks, writhed on the floor. Human bodies, the heads of wolves, reptiles, hyenas, birds of prey.

It was merely pornographic for some time and then it suddenly turned brutal. The masks were torn off two of the women, knives appeared . . .

Julian closed his eyes, shutting out the blood. But the screams went on and on. And then he shouted. The projector was turned off. They sat quietly in the near-darkness. Julian, his eyes still closed, the screams ringing on in his mind, fumbled until he found the cognac snifter.

"You never saw this thing, kid," Callaghan said quietly. "I think it's best for the both of us if we forget all about this."

And Julian had forgotten. But Callaghan had not; he obviously had stolen the reels and attempted to blackmail Saukel and DiMotta.

Saukel's mask had been torn off during the victim's struggles. And Julian could not be sure, but he believed that the three hominids and Neil had also been there, behind the masks. DiMotta, of course, had been the photographer.

It was late afternoon now. Sharon was sleeping. The air was sultry and still. Some low greasy swells were now rolling in from the southwest, forerunners of a storm.

Callaghan, with his whiskey-confidence and whiskey-carelessness, had relaxed his vigilance after exchanging the film reels for evidence that the deposit had been made in his bank account. He'd believed that he was safe then, that it was over. The fool.

Julian heard the cabin cruiser's engines. The big boat, top heavy and rolling, carved a path through the sea, turned and, engines reversed for a moment, eased in alongside the skiff. The two boats bumped lightly. DiMotta was at the flying bridge controls; Saukel, still wearing the terrycloth robe and the ridiculous paper hat, sat in a fishing chair.

DiMotta lifted his right hand, showing Julian a revolver, and then switched off the engines.

The boat's brightwork reflected red from the sunset. The topsides were streaked with salt. Ahead of the cabin, on the foredeck, the dinghy had come loose from its lashing.

Sharon slowly emerged from her sun-drugged lassitude; she lifted her eyes to glance at Julian, straightened, and turned to look over her right shoulder at DiMotta.

Her chalky lips moved soundlessly for an instant, and then there was a crackling sound in her throat and she was saying, "... and haven't you loathesome insects at least the decency to let us die in private?" Her voice was husky but strong.

"Impudent wretch!" Saukel cried, laughing. "Did you hear, Alfredo, insects."

DiMotta calmly looked down at her. One side of his face was swollen and bruised, the other side normal; it looked like a composite face, as if two men's heads had been cleaved and diverse halves cemented together.

Finally DiMotta said, "I think that by tomorrow morning you will at last be prepared to accept direction, Sharon." He could not fully articulate his jaw, and so the words were slurred.

"How obscene you are!" Sharon said scornfully. "Both of you, you and your faggoty buffoon father."

"Medusa!" Saukel cried. And then he quickly became solemn, priestlike. "Crush her, my son."

"DiMotta," Julian said, "I remember seeing the murder film."

DiMotta, one of his eyes partially closed by swelling, stared at him. One corner of his mouth hooked in a smile.

"Callaghan found the film by accident, he showed it to me. I remember it now."

"Oh, Julian, dear boy," Saukel crooned, "we've always known that you were Callaghan's partner. The servants told me you were at the house the day when the reels were stolen."

"I had nothing to do with the theft or the blackmail."

"None of this matters," DiMotta said impatiently.

"What does matter to you? Death?"

He shrugged. "What can possibly concern a serious man more than death? Death is the source of all magic.

Death is power. And the mystery within the mystery, the heart of silence, is exposed—for an instant only—in the ritual of gratuitous murder.''

"More of your bullshit abstractions," Julian said.

Saukel rose to his feet, raised a skeleton hand. "You are right, my boy. Alfredo must always mystify. Murder is evil. But who does not secretly wish to be wholly evil at least once? It cures insomnia, it piques the appetite, it loosens the bowels, it makes me feel young again."

"Frederick must clown as, he says, I must mystify," DiMotta said. "But there is truth in his talk of renewed youth. Perhaps Frederick's participation in murder was an unconscious attempt to expel the death within him by a purging, violent act of transference."

"Zoo time," Sharon said.

He smiled again with one eye and one side of his mouth. "You are aware that many primitive peoples believe that to kill a noble enemy confers his nobility onto the killer. Often the victor will eat his vanquished opponent's heart, brain, and testicles. Courage, wisdom, potency. And recall the once prevalent custom of human sacrifice; one or a few die in order to spare the many. And there you have the Christ myth, do you not? And the Eucharist—Grace attained through cannibalism, eating the flesh and drinking the blood of a god. Power through death. Even salvation through death. And regard the vampire and werewolf myths. Frederick in his way, and I in mine, are telling you some small truths about death. They should have some interest for you, should they not? Since your own deaths are imminent? But perhaps your concern is more immediate, less philosophical. Yes?"

"Can you believe this freak?" Sharon said. "Even now he has to proselytize."

He smiled with one half of his face. "Am I boring you, Sharon?"

"Of course. You always bore me, Alfredo, you know that."

"Yes. You know, Sharon, in a way I love you."

"You have an odd way of showing it."

"Perhaps. But as Nietzsche said, 'What is done out of love always takes place beyond good and evil.' I cultivate an indifference to pain by inflicting pain. I hope to become contemptuous of death by inflicting death. I shall eliminate all hope, all fear. I'll empty myself as one might empty water from a vessel. Then, perhaps, freedom is possible. And with freedom, truth; with truth the key to the only fully lived life; and with life . . . who knows? God?" He smiled again.

"Just go away," Sharon said tiredly. "And leave poor Nietzsche and poor God alone."

"The radio reports that a major storm front is heading in this direction. Frederick and I shall probably have to leave you by noon tomorrow. I only came over here to make you an offer, Sharon. Your life. If you will kill Julian—I'll provide the means—then I will spare you. Think about it tonight and we can discuss it further in the morning. Kill Julian, Sharon, and you will live, I promise it."

He started the engines and the boat slowly pulled away.

---

t w e n t y - o n e

By dusk Julian's pain was almost gone; all that remained was the original burning seed behind his eyes.
He could think clearly now, although he still felt physically weak. He believed that the weakness was due as
much to a lack of exercise as to their having had no
food and very little fluid in more than forty-eight hours.
Except for the short swim yesterday, they had hardly
moved. And there was the heat too, of course; that white,
draining sun, the motionless sultry air.

They drank the rest of the water. Sharon had a twelve-
ounce beer can full, cut one third with salt water; Julian,
a can cut half and half.

"Did you observe much when we sailed, Sharon?"
he asked. "The principles, the mechanics of it?"

She shook her head. The flesh around her eyes was

puffy, but elsewhere the skin seemed to have sunken in close to the bone; hollow cheeks, lumpy cheekbones, a sharply defined jawline. Her neck appeared to be too thin to support the weight of her head.

He explained some of the basic principles and techniques of sailing; the airfoil, management of the sheets and halyards, trimming the sails on various points of sailing, tacking and jibbing, how to reef the main.

"But it's best if you don't fight the wind," he said. "There is land both east and west. Don't take the wind forward of the beam. Do you understand? By the looks of the sky and swells, the wind will be coming out of the southwest—more south than west. If you point a little to the southeast you should have a beam reach all the way to the mainland. But there'll be swells coming from the same direction as the wind, and if they're big you should quarter into them, that'll mean pointing—"

"What are you talking about?" she said suddenly.

"I'm trying to teach you how to handle the boat."

"But why?"

"In case I don't get back tonight."

"What are you going to do?"

"I've got to try something."

"What? Julian, what are you going to try?"

"I don't know exactly," he said. "Take over their boat if I can. Disable it somehow. I won't know what I can do until I swim over there tonight."

"No, please, stay with me."

"You can be ready to sail if anything goes wrong."

"Don't leave me alone here. I'll go with you. I'm a good swimmer, you know I am."

"Did you understand what I was saying before?"

"No, none of it."

"I'll go through all of it again. Listen this time, it may save your life."

Night now. Stars and planets appeared, one by one at first, later in small clusters, and then the entire sky was hazed with bright pinpoint lights. At nine o'clock a poisonous red-hued moon appeared. The sea duplicated the Milky Way star for star and scattered broken pieces of moonlight all around. And beneath the water's surface there was still another cosmos; sparkling phosphorescent stars and planets, spray-tailed comets that arced and died, hovering globes of green light, meteors, and supernovas.

"What are you thinking about?" he asked Sharon. "DiMotta's offer?"

"Julian!"

"Were you?"

"It's unthinkable."

"No, it isn't. I was thinking about it."

"Well, I wasn't."

"It was very clever of DiMotta."

"It was horrible."

"And I really believe that he meant it, Sharon. He actually would spare your life if you killed me tomorrow. He could even return to the resort tomorrow as a hero—one of the lost mariners unfortunately perished, but the other survived and was saved."

"That's stupid. Please, I don't want to talk about this."

"DiMotta would have the murder on film, of course. You couldn't very well go to the police and tell them that you had killed me in order to save your own life. It would be absolutely true, perhaps even justifiable—after all, I'd be a dead man anyway. But you would be indicted for murder. No, DiMotta would let you go, it would stimulate his sense of humor to see you kill me, and maybe confirm him in his viewpoint of human nature."

Sharon watched him silently.

"He presented you with the classic double bind. Damned if you do and dead if you don't. The days out here, the isolation and hardship, the fear, thirst, all of that. He's counting on a breakdown of your personality, of course. And this one more long night of suffering and fear before you are given your alternatives—live or die."

She was slowly shaking her head.

"That's one aspect," he continued. "There is another; this is a double double bind. Because—according to DiMotta's thinking—there is a very good chance that *I* would murder *you* tonight. You see? I might be expected to be somewhat deranged too. If I really believed that you would murder me tomorrow, why . . ."

"I hate the way you're talking to me," she said. "I would never do it, Julian, and you know that."

"I know it. But say that I fail to take over or disable the cabin cruiser tonight and yet still make it back to the skiff. Both of us will die tomorrow unless . . . unless perhaps I commit suicide at your hand. Do you see? If I consent in my death, take the moral responsibility upon my self, authorize you—no, *plead* with you to kill me . . ."

"What's happened to you? Have you gone crazy?"

"There are a couple of pencils in the toolbox and some paperback books. I could write a note on the blank pages explaining that, in effect, I died by my own hand. Why should both of us die when one can live? You could maybe go to the police then, if you chose. There would still be a trial, but a jury just might let you off."

"Stop," she said. "Just stop now."

"Okay. But if I am willing to do it, Sharon, you at least ought to consider the idea."

They sat together in silence for a long time, and then

Julian fell asleep. It was close to midnight when he awakened and saw that the sea was coldly flaming. The previous nights' phosphorescence was nothing compared to this; the sea blazed with life. Millions of green dots flashed beneath the surface; in some areas they were packed so close together that they composed solid balls of light. And there were thicker, longer streaks, and blurs and parabolas. Fish jumped all around the boat, and he saw a dark shape, wreathed in the greenish light, that was two-thirds as long as the skiff.

He leaned over the side, scooped up one of the small lights with his cupped palms, and dropped it into the skiff. It looked like a cockroach, perhaps a scorpion. He struck his cigarette lighter and held it close to the animal. It was only a shrimp. Hordes of shrimp had approached the surface for some reason, and fish of all sizes had gathered to feed upon them.

He looked toward the northwest. The hull of the cabin cruiser had fallen below the short night horizon, but the superstructure and outriggers remained silhouetted against the sky. Huge cauliflower-shaped clouds were massing to the south. Some thin, sooty clouds, like scouts for the army left behind, were streaming overhead, momentarily dimming the moon and stars. The swells were larger. And there was a gusty breeze now; it would be possible to sail.

"Sharon."

She awakened immediately, looked at him for a time, and then turned to the sea. "What's happening?"

"Shrimp," he said. "Millions of them."

"You're not going into the water with them."

"There are no man-eating shrimp in this longitude," he said lightly.

"But there are other fish out there. You can see them splash."

"I'm going."

"But look how far away their boat is. It's much too far, wait until they bring it closer."

"They might drift another two miles. They might not be this close to us for the rest of the night."

"Are you really going?"

"Yes."

"All right, then. What do you want me to do?"

"I'm leaving you my watch and cigarette lighter. If I'm not back in forty minutes, stand up and flash it at intervals. Let it burn for a few seconds, let it go out, then fire it again. That way I'll know it isn't a star."

She nodded.

"And if I'm not back in fifty minutes you can figure that you're on your own. You decide then, sail right away or wait for the wind and seas to pick up, the clouds to come in. Run hard for several miles and then try to change course. If you can get beyond their radar range and then alter directions, you've got a damned good chance."

"Okay."

"Hey, don't cry," he said.

"I can't help it. I'm sorry."

He got the small rusty jackknife from the toolbox and put it into the pocket of his shorts. He decided to wear his shirt; it might provide a little insulation from the cold water.

"I'll give you an hour," she said. "An hour, not fifty minutes."

"Okay." He looked for the Big Dipper, found it, and that led his eye to Polaris. Polaris would be on his left as he swam west toward the cabin cruiser; on his right when he returned.

Julian kissed Sharon lightly on her cheek, tasted the

salt tears. She embraced him tightly, was unwilling to let go, but finally she relaxed.

He slipped over the side. The swells seemed much bigger when he entered the water; the skiff lifted swiftly, tugging at his arm, and then began to drop. He released his grip and a space opened between him and the boat. He was aware of the flashes his legs and arms made as he treaded water.

A fish broke the surface a few yards away. Something brushed his side, another something touched his leg. He had expected contact with the shrimp and had believed himself prepared, but still he nearly cried out. It was the not seeing, the not being certain what was down there. He was immersed in a great green galaxy of light, and he knew that for every single glow there was movement, a creature disturbing the plankton.

He waited until a swell lifted him to its summit, saw the cabin cruiser, and began swimming. Shrimp touched his body at every stroke. He was glad he had worn the shirt. Each touch was a violation of both his body and psyche, both recoiled.

He swam twenty-five strokes, rested for a count of thirty, went on.

A fish hit his thigh. It was small, he knew that almost immediately, no more than a few pounds; but the impact was like a prolonged electrical shock. Julian heard himself groan, a rumbling, alien sound.

He touched his cut thigh; a rough, circular wound about the size of a half dollar, loose shreds of skin. He did not believe that it had been a deliberate attack; the fish had struck at a shrimp, missed and hit him.

The cabin cruiser was still a long swim away, perhaps one hundred and twenty yards or so. Red lights burned behind the curtained windows. It rolled uneasily, beam on to the swells, and when descending into the troughs the water around it glowed brightly.

As he looked back now, all he could see of the skiff was the mast, and that only when the skiff was poised high on a wave. The mast was cocked at a thirty-degree angle. Nothing for half a minute, and then the mast was again outlined against the sky, tilted thirty degrees in the other direction.

He went on, already tired. The past two days had drained his strength even more than he had assumed. And the water, which had felt warm at first, a soothing salt bath, now chilled him. He realized that he should have given himself more time. Sixty minutes, Sharon had said, increasing his own limit by ten minutes. Sixty minutes might not have been enough even if he had been in perfect health.

Twenty-five strokes, a rest of half a minute, twenty-five strokes. He was losing his coordination.

When the cabin cruiser was close he could smell gasoline and oil. The red cabin lights were still burning. Red would not affect DiMotta's night vision; he could come out on deck and see well, would not have to wait for his eyes to adjust to the darkness.

He waited until a cloud passed beneath the moon and then swam closer. He saw now that it would be very difficult to climb aboard; DiMotta had blocked the cut-down transom with the cruiser's ten-foot dinghy, lashed it tightly to cleats and railing stanchions. There was no opening. And too, the swells had imparted enormous power to the inert mass of the boat, converted its fifteen tons into an effective weight of thirty tons, more. The water around it boiled. There was a sound like breaking surf. The seas, which had seemed so harmless to Julian while he swam, now revealed their true strength as they met an object that partly resisted them. Simply holding

on to that plunging giant would be difficult and dangerous. To climb aboard . . .

Julian watched the boat for a time, gauging its
rhythms. Then he timed the swells, began counting when
atop one and stopped when he had risen to the crest of
the next. Fourteen seconds. The cabin cruiser dropped
and then ascended eight or nine vertical feet during that
time.

He swam to within a few feet of the stern, waited in
the seething green tumult. A swell was passing on beneath them. Julian timed the roll, and when the starboard
end of the stern was at its lowest point he reached up
with one hand and grabbed the base of a stanchion, held
on. The boat began to roll the other way, lifting him
halfway out of the water. There was a popping sound in
his right shoulder. He got his other hand on the stanchion, pulled himself upward. The boat was at the high
point of its roll now. He was free of the water. He
strained. The boat was beginning its reverse roll. He
brought his legs up, placed his feet flat against the transom and levered his upper body over the edge. Then it
was only a matter of doing a slow, controlled somersault
onto the deck.

twenty-two

Exhausted, he sat sprawled on the wet deck, listening to the ripping hiss of wind and seas, feeling his body rise heavily and then almost weightlessly descend. A sharp smell of gasoline. Cold, pain.

After a brief rest Julian got up and lightly crossed the deck to a cabin portlight. The curtains had not been fully drawn; there was a narrow slit in the center.

DiMotta, his swollen face unshaven, and Saukel, vulturine, were on opposite sides of the swing table, hunched over a chess board.

The cabin interior was suffused with a dim light from three red-glassed oil lamps hung in gimbals. DiMotta was conserving the batteries. Perhaps he did not want to waste any more fuel charging them; they must be running a little low on gasoline by now.

DiMotta sat stiffly, tense even now, resisting the motion, while Saukel—that rubbery giant—submitted, his head bobbing this way and that as if it too were set in gimbals.

The crimson light was reflected off all of the polished surfaces in the cabin, the bronze and mahogany and stainless steel. It was a distorting light, appearing to shorten and widen the cabin in the same way that certain camera lenses would.

Saukel's jaw split as his lips—purplish red in the light—spread in a V-smile. He waited for a moment of equilibrium in the boat's tossing, his hand dangling clawlike over the board, and then moved one of his bishops.

DiMotta glanced up briefly, then returned his attention to the board.

So then, here they were, bellies full, and nearby a lever that with half a twist would gush fresh water out of a pipe. Enjoying a tough game of chess. Port and cashews later, maybe, or cognac. And all the while aware that within a few hundred yards . . .

Julian stepped away from the window and prowled the deck for a weapon. There was the boat hook, but it was too long to get easily through the narrow doorway and, once inside, to wield effectively.

His attack must be swift. One of the aluminum rods used to erect the cockpit awning?—too light. He found a rusty crescent wrench in the bottom of the dinghy; it too was a little light, but with a properly aimed blow to the head . . .

He returned to the window. DiMotta had not changed positions; Saukel was smoking a cigar now, the threads of smoke twisting up to the ceiling and then flattening. Watching them, Julian reached over and cautiously tested the bronze door lever. It moved, the door was not locked. Well, then, go. Don't worry about Saukel.

He waited until the boat had completed its roll and was briefly poised atop a swell; and then he twisted the lever, pushed hard, and rushed into the cabin.

There was a frozen microsecond as he passed through the doorway. All action ceased as though a reel of film had suddenly been halted on a single frame. It was almost as if he were photographing the scene; he saw with a camera's eye. The boat was tilted about twenty-five degrees to port, and angled bow-down too; everything except the swing table (with its polished ivory chess pieces) and the gimbaled oil lamps were cocked awry, and even they appeared to negate gravity. The lamps' soft red light created spidery red-gold blurs on the mahogany and bronze, and flowed liquidly into maroon pools. Both DiMotta and Saukel had turned toward him. There had not been time for them to express alarm— two men glancing up at a disturbance that did not much concern them.

DiMotta, compact and handsome despite his swollen jaw; Saukel, teeth clenching a cigar, grotesque. And now Julian saw that DiMotta's revolver was on the settee next to his thigh.

An instant. And then motion resumed, clarity dissolved into confusion and noise, shouts, DiMotta reaching for the gun, Saukel rising, the boat plunging into a trough and reversing its roll, lamps and table swinging, DiMotta now lifting the revolver and Saukel almost erect, and Julian was across the cabin and swinging the wrench.

The blow landed high on the side of DiMotta's head; he stiffened, and almost completed the motion of lifting and aiming the revolver before his eyes glazed and he collapsed sideways onto the settee. Julian twisted the revolver loose from his grip and turned. Saukel had fallen onto his back and lay sprawled full-length, his long limbs writhing buglike as he attempted to rise.

"Stay there," Julian said to him.

Saukel stopped moving. His eyes were wide; his lips twisted. "Please. It was only a silly joke."

"This is a silly joke too," Julian said. "You'll die laughing."

"Julian, please . . . please, son . . . it was all Alfredo's idea . . . I didn't want . . ."

DiMotta had slowly drawn himself to a sitting position. He touched his fingertips to the head wound and then looked at the blood.

"I'm with you," Saukel was saying. "I've been with you all along."

"Will you kill him?" Julian said.

"Yes, yes, give me the gun."

"You'll have to use a knife."

"A knife, then, get me a knife. Oh, I'll do it, boy, gladly, don't believe I won't."

"A dull knife," Julian said.

DiMotta, his eyes closed, was smiling faintly.

"How about you?" Julian said to him. "Will you kill Saukel if I let you live?"

"No!" Saukel cried.

"Will you?"

DiMotta opened his eyes. "I invent games like these, I don't play them."

Julian cocked the revolver.

DiMotta calmly looked over the barrel at Julian's eyes.

"You don't believe I'll pull the trigger?" He moved the muzzle to within a few inches of DiMotta's face. "Watch," he said. "Maybe you'll be able to see it coming."

DiMotta broke then; he winced and closed his eyes, and his face seemed to compress.

"Do it," Saukel said. "Kill him, my boy, pull the trigger. If you can't do it, get me a knife, a dull knife."

DiMotta was very pale. A tic jerked at the corner of his mouth.

"Bang!" Saukel yelled, and then laughed. "Bang!"

"Has death lost some of its charm, Alfredo?"

Julian turned and went forward to the control panel. The key was in the ignition switch. He figured that while the engines were warming he could tie up the two of them—there was always plenty of rope on a boat—and drag them down into the bow cabin. Then he would climb to the controls on the flying bridge and search for Sharon.

He twisted the key.

"The blowers!" DiMotta shouted.

There was a soft whooshing noise as oxygen was sucked to the flames.

"You fool!"

Julian was confused, stunned, and then realized that he had failed to clear the bilges of gasoline fumes and they had ignited from the electrical spark. The boat had turned into a bomb.

He ran across the cabin, out onto the deck and dived overboard. He swam hard, desperately, for forty yards and then looked back. Flames leaped behind the port-lights, erupted from the deck well. It was going to blow; it was a near miracle that it hadn't already exploded. He swam on, anticipating the concussive blast with each stroke, and when he turned he saw that the fire had diminished, was a shivering red glow in the darkness. The cabin cruiser rode easily to the top of a swell and vanished on the other side. When it rose again, he saw that the fire was out or nearly out.

Incredible. The boat should have blown into a thousand flaming pieces. Still, the cabin cruiser had to be disabled now; the electrical wiring could not have survived the fire intact. DiMotta and Saukel were hardly better off than he and Sharon now.

He had lost the revolver. And he was aware that much of the phosphorescence was far below him, dimming as it receded. The shrimp were returning to the bottom.

The skiff. Sharon.

Julian had hardly been aware of the silky touch of the current before, but now, going against it, he found that he had to swim twice as long in order to cover an equivalent distance; ten strokes now, for five before. His shoulders ached; his limbs were numbed by cold and fatigue.

He swam twenty-five strokes and rested for a count of thirty. No good. Fifteen strokes, count to sixty. Still too much. Ten strokes and sixty seconds rest; even that was hard, but he felt capable of continuing for a while at that rate.

During the rests he looked for Polaris, the moon, the cabin cruiser, roughly calculating their relative positions, and then drew an imaginary line that he hoped would intersect the skiff or at least come close. That was the theory. But he doubted that he would ever see the skiff again; it was too small, the seas too large, and visibility was rapidly decreasing as the clouds moved in. And of course the big cabin cruiser and the skiff had been drifting at different rates. The moon was moving; the constellations changed positions. Only Polaris among his reference points remained still.

He knew that he was not going to make it.

But he intended to keep going until he simply could no longer remain afloat. By then, he guessed, his exhaustion would make death quick and not too painful.

He did not fear death very much now; it seemed that his mind had already begun to numb, and he had no strong consciousness of self. He was sure that when the time came to submit, his mind would observe the struggles of his body with nothing more than a remote pity. He hoped it would be that way. He was not afraid of death itself, the eternal sleep, only the process of dying, that last flicker of unbelief.

He was unable to estimate the passage of time. He lost count of his strokes, rested much longer than he had planned, ceased counting. For brief periods he entered a kind of dream state and was only dully aware of where he was, and why, what it was he was attempting. It was like being very drunk.

The cabin cruiser was no longer visible. He was alone, really alone, slipping over into eternity. Soon now.

And then he was surprised to see a small red glow far to his left. The cabin cruiser, burning again? But that boat was far behind. The light appeared again and below it he saw a short, vertical section of mast. A signal light. Perhaps Sharon had set fire to the paperback books in the bail bucket and then hauled the bucket aloft with the mainsail halyard. Smart, smart. The fire dimmed, went out, but he knew where the skiff was now, and he was pretty sure he could swim that much farther.

t w e n t y - t h r e e

Julian steered toward the southeast, quartering into the endless rows of swells. The seas were big, perhaps twenty feet from trough to crest, but far apart and still smoothly rounded. They would steepen as the wind increased, and alter form, and then all of their latent power would be released. Sharon was already frightened—now holding tightly to a thwart and crying out as they skidded down the backside of a wave in a torrent of glittering foam—but conditions would become worse. He had to gamble, though; the thing was to push hard, close to the skiff's and his own limits, run away from DiMotta and toward land. If they could reach the mainland before the storm broke full force . . .

An hour later he put a reef in the mainsail. Clouds boiled across the sky, pushing farther north with each tumbling thrust, quenching stars, the Big Dipper and Polaris. Now Julian's most important navigational reference was gone; all that remained to guide him was the direction of the wind and seas.

"Sing," he said.

There was not yet a great amount of noise; the hum of wind in the standing rigging, the snap of a sailcloth, a fizzing when a whitecap bloomed in the darkness—he did not have to raise his voice.

"Talk to me."

She was lying huddled in the bottom of the skiff, curled around the base of the mast.

"Sharon?"

She stirred. "What?"

"Are you okay?"

"Sick, God, I'm sick. And thirsty and wet and cold."

"Hang on."

"Are we going to make it, Julian?"

"Sure," he said.

Later it rained, a few cold drops driven horizontally by the wind at first, and then a downpour that silvered the dark sea and drummed against the sails. Sharon, using the bail can, collected rainwater as it drained off the tack of the mainsail. They drank all they could hold, and ten minutes later were thirsty again.

The wind was stronger now; he had Sharon lower the jib and they sailed on under reefed mainsail alone.

It rained, lightning skittered lizardlike across the clouds, and every now and then in the darkness he saw the thundering white cataract of a breaking swell. He was confused by the globe of chaos; everywhere, constantly, shadows rose and fell and rose again, advanced and retreated, lunged wildly, and the harder gusts of wind pressed the skiff over until water rushed in over the gunwale.

"Bail!" he shouted.

It was coming down to luck now. He was sailing at the limits of his reflexes and skill, beyond. And the boat, poorly balanced under the reefed mainsail, was heavy on the tiller and had a tendency to skew sideways while surfing down into the troughs. They could die half a dozen different ways now; broaching, getting buried by a breaking swell, equipment breakage, steering error, the skiff getting knocked down by a sudden wind gust. . . . It was as though dice were being rolled continually and they had to come up winners every time.

Later, five minutes or an hour (he was no longer capable of estimating time), he noticed that Sharon was staring intently at him, her lips moving.

"What?"

She pointed. "It's getting light."

He believed that she was imagining the light, but then slowly, imperceptibly, details began to emerge out of the darkness.

The perimeter of his vision steadily expanded; he could see thirty feet, fifty, a hundred yards, a half mile, a mile. Ahead, a low smudge on the horizon. Cloud? Land?

And then Sharon cried out and pointed toward the south, a boat, and behind it, another. And one to the west that looked as though it would pass within two or three hundred yards. Shrimp trawlers, running into port.

The trawler to the west slowly approached, trembling violently amidst diagonal explosions of foam, drew even, went past, and then suddenly began to turn. A figure appeared on deck; then two more. One of the men waved.

While Sharon was in the shower, he called room service and ordered two big breakfasts, eggs and ham and potatoes and toast, a pot of coffee; and cigarettes and a bottle of brandy.

Now Julian stood in front of the sliding glass doors and looked out at the storm. The wind had increased, doubled, it seemed, and struck with a violence that shook the building and whipped the sea into a heaving froth. Palms curved almost double. Beach sand erupted and streamed away in smoky clouds.

Sharon, wrapped in a terrycloth towel, walked barefoot across the carpet and stood next to him. Her hair was darkly wet, her skin still damp, and she smelled of perfumed soap.

"We're safe," she said. "I can hardly believe it, we're finally safe."

"We were lucky."

"And brave. Weren't we brave, Julian?"

"Yes, I guess we were at that."

"And are we going to continue being brave?"

"There's not much choice."

"Brave together?"

He nodded.

She was silent for a time and then said, "God, just look at that . . . that . . ."

"Maelstrom."

"Yes, maelstrom. I wonder how DiMotta's movie is proceeding out there in the maelstrom."

epilogue

239— **Day, exterior.** The CAMERA PANS the stormy sea. Driven rain and spray have obscured the horizon; it is hard to differentiate between sea and sky.

240— **Day, exterior.** CAMERA PANS the visible length of a huge black wave. It is streaked with lateral lines of foam and SOUNDS like swarming bees.

241— **Day, exterior.** In SLOW MOTION we see the wave rise high above us. Spume is torn off the tumbling crest. The wave reaches its critical point, balance surrenders to chaos, and a roaring cataract of white water rushes toward us. The CAMERA is inundated.

242— **Day, exterior.** CAMERA PANS, revealing, at

different angles, the furious tumult, the thrusting and collapsing sea mountains.

243— **Day, exterior.** CAMERA PANS, closing its 360° revolution. CAMERA HALTS and we see a dark object, which is not immediately recognizable in the gray distance. The object vanishes behind an avalanching wave.

244— **Day, exterior.** The CAMERA MOVES in the direction of the vanished object. We climb the froth-streaked waves and swoop down into the troughs. The object reappears and we now see that it is a boat.

245— **Day, exterior.** LONG SHOT of the disabled boat. There seem to be two figures moving about in the well behind the cabin.

246— **Day, exterior.** MEDIUM SHOT of the boat. (The SOUND of the wind, wailing flute notes before, rises to a shrill whistling scream as it is deflected by the angled surfaces of the boat.) The two men, secured by ropes, are frantically levering the handles of the bilge pumps. A breaking wave buries the boat.

247— **Day, exterior.** CAMERA LOOKS DOWN as the boat struggles to right itself and shed the tons of foaming water. It does rise finally, but its motion is slower now, sluggish, and begins to greet the seas at a different angle. The two men slowly rise, first one, and then very slowly, the other. They stagger back to their pumping stations.

248— **Day, exterior.** CLOSE UP of the younger man.

249— **Day, exterior.** CLOSE UP of the older man.

250— **Day, exterior.** CAMERA LOOKS DOWN. CAMERA RISES and below we see the boat and the two men. The lumpy sea is windscaled and oddly crosshatched with white: the east-west lines are the tumbling crests of the swells; the north-south lines are the thick, wind-driven streamers of foam. The boat gets smaller, and the sea smoother-looking, as the CAMERA RISES. It is absolutely silent now. The CAMERA RISES into cloud. We see the boat and its tiny human figures through a thickening veil of mist, and then it is gone. SLOW DISSOLVE.

Available by mail from

PEOPLE OF THE LIGHTNING • Kathleen O'Neal Gear and W. Michael Gear

The next novel in the First North American series by best-selling authors Kathleen O'Neal Gear and W. Michael Gear.

RELIC • Douglas Preston and Lincoln Child

Alien meets *Jurassic Park* in New York City!

MAGNIFICENT SAVAGES • Fred Mustard Stewart

From China's opium trade to Garibaldi's Italy to the New York of Astor and Vanderbilt, comes this blockbuster, 19th century historical novel of the clipper ships and the men who made them.

WORLD WITHOUT END • Molly Cochran and Warren Murphy

"In this exciting adventure the mysterious island is artfully combined with the Bermuda Triangle and modern day life."—VOYA

A MAN'S GAME • Newton Thornburg

Another startling thriller from the author of *Cutter and Bone*, which *The New York Times* called "the best novel of its kind in ten years!"

SPOOKER • Dean Ing

It took the government a long time to figure out that someone was killing agents for their spookers—until that someone made one fatal mistake.

WHITE SMOKE • Andrew M. Greeley

Only Andrew M. Greeley, Catholic priest and bestselling novelist, could have written this blockbuster tale about what *might* happen when the next Pope must be chosen and the fate of the Church itself hangs in the balance.